Hangman's Holiday

◆

Other mysteries by Dorothy L. Sayers:

DOROTHY L. SAYERS

Hangman's Holiday

·

PERENNIAL LIBRARY

Harper & Row, Publishers, New York
Cambridge, Philadelphia, San Francisco, Washington
London, Mexico City, São Paulo, Singapore, Sydney

Library of Congress Cataloging-in-Publication Data

Sayers, Dorothy L. (Dorothy Leigh), 1893–1957.
  Hangman's holiday.

  Reprint. Originally published: New York: Harcourt,
Brace, Jovanovich, 1933.
    1. Detective and mystery stories, English.   2. Wimsey,
Peter, Lord (Fictitious character)—Fiction.   I. Title.
PR6037.A95H28   1987   823'.912   86-45691
ISBN 0-06-055033-3   87 88 89 90   HC 9 8 7 6 5 4 3 2 1
ISBN 0-06-080837-3 (pbk.)   '92 OPM 9 8 7 6 5 4

CONTENTS

♦

Lord Peter Wimsey Stories

Montague Egg Stories

Other Stories

AUTHOR'S NOTE

◆

EVERY person, incident, institution, college, firm or whatnot in this book is purely imaginary and is not intended to refer to any actual person, incident, institution, college, firm or whatnot whatsoever.

Part One

___

LORD PETER WIMSEY STORIES
◆

CHAPTER I

•

The Image in the Mirror

The little man with the cow-lick seemed so absorbed in the book that Wimsey had not the heart to claim his property, but, drawing up the other arm-chair and placing his drink within easy reach, did his best to entertain himself with the Dunlop Book, which graced, as usual, one of the tables in the lounge.

The little man read on, his elbows squared upon the arms of his chair, his ruffled red head bent anxiously over the text. He breathed heavily, and when he came to the turn of the page, he set the thick volume down on his knee and used both hands for his task. Not what is called "a great reader," Wimsey decided.

When he reached the end of the story, he turned laboriously back, and read one passage over again with attention. Then he laid the book, still open, upon the table, and in so doing caught Wimsey's eye.

"I beg your pardon, sir," he said in his rather thin Cockney voice, "is this your book?"

"It doesn't matter at all," said Wimsey graciously, "I know it by heart. I only brought it along with me because it's handy for reading a few pages when you're stuck in a place like this for the night. You can always take it up and find something entertaining."

"This chap Wells," pursued the red-haired man, "he's what you'd call a very clever writer, isn't he? It's wonderful how he makes it all so real, and yet some of the things he says, you wouldn't hardly think they could be really possible. Take this story now; would you say, sir, a thing like that could actually happen to a person, as it might be you—or me?"

Wimsey twisted his head round so as to get a view of the page.

3

"*The Plattner Experiment*," he said, "that's the one about the schoolmaster who was blown into the fourth dimension and came back with his right and left sides reversed. Well, no, I don't suppose such a thing would really occur in real life, though of course it's very fascinating to play with the idea of a fourth dimension."

"Well—" He paused and looked up shyly at Wimsey. "I don't rightly understand about this fourth dimension. I didn't know there was such a place, but he makes it all very clear no doubt to them that know science. But this right-and-left business, now, I know that's a fact. By experience, if you'll believe me."

Wimsey extended his cigarette-case. The little man made an instinctive motion towards it with his left hand and then seemed to check himself and stretched his right across.

"There, you see. I'm always left-handed when I don't think about it. Same as this Plattner. I fight against it, but it doesn't seem any use. But I wouldn't mind that—it's a small thing and plenty of people are left-handed and think nothing of it. No. It's the dretful anxiety of not knowing what I mayn't be doing when I'm in this fourth dimension or whatever it is."

He sighed deeply.

"I'm worried, that's what I am, worried to death."

"Suppose you tell me about it, said Wimsey."

"I don't like telling people about it, because they might think I had a slate loose. But it's fairly getting on my nerves. Every morning when I wake up I wonder what I've been doing in the night and whether it's the day of the month it ought to be. I can't get any peace till I see the morning paper, and even then I can't be sure. . . .

"Well, I'll tell you, if you won't take it as a bore or a liberty. It all began—" He broke off and glanced nervously about the room. "There's nobody to see. If you wouldn't mind, sir, putting your hand just here a minute—"

He unbuttoned his rather regrettable double-breasted waistcoat, and laid a hand on the part of his anatomy usually considered to indicate the site of the heart.

"By all means," said Wimsey, doing as he was requested.

"Do you feel anything?"

4

"I don't know that I do," said Wimsey. "What ought I to feel? A swelling or anything? If you mean your pulse, the wrist is a better place."

"Oh, you can feel it *there*, all right," said the little man. "Just try the other side of the chest, sir."

Wimsey obediently moved his hand across.

"I seem to detect a little flutter," he said after a pause.

"You do? Well, you wouldn't expect to find it that side and not the other, would you? Well, that's where it is. I've got my heart on the right side, that's what I wanted you to feel for yourself."

"Did it get displaced in an illness?" asked Wimsey sympathetically.

"In a manner of speaking. But that's not all. My liver's got round the wrong side, too, and my organs. I've had a doctor see it, and he told me I was all reversed. I've got my appendix on my left side—that is, I had till they took it away. If we was private, now, I could show you the scar. It was a great surprise to the surgeon when they told him about me. He said afterwards it made it quite awkward for him, coming left-handed to the operation, as you might say."

"It's unusual, certainly," said Wimsey, "but I believe such cases do occur sometimes."

"Not the way it occurred to me. It happened in an air-raid."

"In an air-raid?" said Wimsey, aghast.

"Yes—and if that was all it had done to me I'd put up with it and be thankful. Eighteen I was then, and I'd just been called up. Previous to that I'd been working in the packing department at Crichton's—you've heard of them, I expect—Crichton's for Admirable Advertising, with offices in Holborn. My mother was living in Brixton, and I'd come up to town on leave from the training-camp. I'd been seeing one or two of my old pals, and I thought I'd finish the evening by going to see a film at the Stoll. It was after supper—I had just time to get in to the last house, so I cut across from Leicester Square through Covent Garden Market. Well, I was getting along when wallop! A bomb came down it seemed to me right under my feet, and everything went black for a bit."

5

"That was the raid that blew up Oldham's, I suppose."

"Yes, it was January 28th, 1918. Well, as I say, everything went right out. Next thing as I knew, I was walking in some place in broad daylight, with green grass all round me, and trees, and water to the side of me, and knowing no more about how I got there than the man in the moon."

"Good Lord!" said Wimsey. "And was it the fourth dimension, do you think?"

"Well, no, it wasn't. It was Hyde Park, as I come to see when I had my wits about me. I was along the bank of the Serpentine and there was a seat with some women sitting on it, and children playing about."

"Had the explosion damaged you?"

"Nothing to see or feel, except that I had a big bruise on one hip and shoulder as if I'd been chucked up against something. I was fairly staggered. The air-raid had gone right out of my mind, don't you see, and I couldn't imagine how I came there, and why I wasn't at Crichton's. I looked at my watch, but that had stopped. I was feeling hungry. I felt in my pocket and found some money there, but it wasn't as much as I should have had—not by a long way. But I felt I must have a bit of something, so I got out of the Park by the Marble Arch gate, and went into a Lyons. I ordered two poached on toast and a pot of tea, and while I was waiting I took up a paper that somebody had left on the seat. Well, that finished me. The last thing I remembered was starting off to see that film on the 28th—and here was the date on the paper—January 30th! I'd lost a whole day and two nights somewhere!"

"Shock," suggested Wimsey. The little man took the suggestion and put his own meaning on it.

"Shock? I should think it was. I was scared out of my life. The girl who brought my eggs must have thought I was barmy. I asked her what day of the week it was, and she said 'Friday.' There wasn't any mistake.

"Well, I don't want to make this bit too long, because that's not the end by a long chalk. I got my meal down somehow, and went to see a doctor. He asked me what I remembered doing last, and I told him about the film, and he asked whether I was out in the air-raid. Well, then it came back to me, and

I remembered the bomb falling, but nothing more. He said I'd had a nervous shock and lost my memory a bit, and that it often happened and I wasn't to worry. And then he said he'd look me over to see if I'd got hurt at all. So he started in with his stethoscope, and all of a sudden he said to me:

"'Why, you keep your heart on the wrong side, my lad!'

"'Do I?' said I. 'That's the first I've heard of it.'

"Well, he looked me over pretty thoroughly, and then he told me what I've told you, that I was all reversed inside, and he asked a lot of questions about my family. I told him I was an only child and my father was dead—killed by a motor-lorry, he was, when I was a kid of ten—and I lived with my mother in Brixton and all that. And he said I was an unusual case, but there was nothing to worry about. Bar being wrong side round I was sound as a bell, and he told me to go home and take things quietly for a day or two.

"Well, I did, and I felt all right, and I thought that was the end of it, though I'd overstayed my leave and had a bit of a job explaining myself to the R.T.O. It wasn't till several months afterwards the draft was called up, and I went along for my farewell leave. I was having a cup of coffee in the Mirror Hall at the Strand Corner House—you know it, down the steps?"

Wimsey nodded.

"All the big looking-glasses all round. I happened to look into the one near me, and I saw a young lady smiling at me as if she knew me. I saw her reflection, that is, if you understand me. Well, I couldn't make it out, for I had never seen her before, and I didn't take any notice, thinking she'd mistook me for somebody else. Besides, though I wasn't so very old then, I thought I knew her sort, and my mother had always brought me up strict. I looked away and went on with my coffee, and all of a sudden a voice said quite close to me:

"'Hullo, Ginger—aren't you going to say good evening?'

"I looked up and there she was. Pretty, too, if she hadn't been painted up so much.

"'I'm afraid,' I said, rather stiff, 'you have the advantage of me, miss.'

7

"'Oh, Ginger,' says she, 'Mr. Duckworthy, and after Wednesday night!' A kind of mocking way she had of speaking.

"I hadn't thought so much of her calling me Ginger, because that's what any girl would say to a fellow with my sort of hair, but when she got my name off so pat, I tell you it did give me a turn.

"'You seem to think we're acquainted, miss,' said I.

"'Well, I should rather say so, shouldn't you?' said she.

"There! I needn't go into it all. From what she said I found out she thought she'd met me one night and taken me home with her. And what frightened me most of all, she said it had happened on the night of the big raid.

"'It *was* you,' she said, staring into my face a little puzzled-like. 'Of course it was you. I knew you in a minute when I saw your face in the glass.'

"Of course, I couldn't say that it hadn't been. I knew no more of what I'd been and done that night than the babe unborn. But it upset me cruelly, because I was an innocent sort of lad in those days and hadn't ever gone with girls, and it seemed to me if I'd done a thing like that I ought to know about it. It seemed to me I'd been doing wrong and not getting full value for my money either.

"I made some excuse to get rid of her, and I wondered what else I'd been doing. She couldn't tell me farther than the morning of the 29th, and it worried me a bit wondering if I'd done any other queer things."

"It must have," said Wimsey, and put his finger on the bell. When the waiter arrived, he ordered drinks for two and disposed himself to listen to the rest of Mr. Duckworthy's adventures.

"I didn't think much about it, though," went on the little man; "we went abroad, and I saw my first corpse and dodged my first shell and had my first dose of trenches, and I hadn't much time for what they call introspection.

"The next queer thing that happened was in the C.C.S. at Ytres. I'd got a blighty one near Caudry in September during the advance from Cambrai—half buried, I was, in a mine explosion and laid out unconscious near twenty-four hours it must have been. When I came to, I was wandering about somewhere behind the lines with a nasty hole in my shoulder. Somebody had bandaged it up for me, but I hadn't any recollection of that. I walked a long way, not knowing where I was, till at last I fetched up in an aid-post. They fixed me up and sent me down the line to a base hospital. I was pretty feverish, and the next thing I knew, I was in bed with a nurse looking after me. The bloke in the next bed to mine was asleep. I got talking to a chap in the next bed beyond him, and he told me where I was, when all of a sudden the other man woke up and says:

"'My God,' he says, 'you dirty ginger-haired swine, it's you, is it? What have you done with them vallables?'

"I tell you, I was struck all of a heap. Never seen the man in my life. But he went on at me and made such a row, the nurse came running in to see what was up. All the men were sitting up in bed listening—you never saw anything like it.

"The upshot was, as soon as I could understand what this fellow was driving at, that he'd been sharing a shell-hole with a chap that he said was me, and that this chap and he had talked together a bit and then, when he was weak and helpless, the chap had looted his money and watch and revolver and what not and gone off with them. A nasty, dirty trick, and I couldn't blame him for making a row about it, if true. But I said and stood to it, it wasn't me, but some other fellow of the same man. He said he recognised me—said he and this other chap had been together a whole day, and he knew every feature in his face and couldn't be mistaken. However, it seemed this bloke had said he belonged to the Blankshires, and I was able to show my papers and prove I belonged to the Buffs, and eventually the bloke apologized and said he must have made a mistake. He died, anyhow, a few days after, and we all agreed he must have been wandering a bit. The two divisions were fighting side by side in that dust-up and it was possible for them to get mixed up. I tried afterwards to find out whether by any chance I had a double in the Blankshires, but they sent me back home, and before I was fit again the Armistice was signed, and I didn't take any more trouble.

"I went back to my old job after the war, and things seemed to settle down a bit. I got engaged when I was twenty-one to

9

a regular good girl, and I thought everything in the garden was lovely. And then, one day—up it all went! My mother was dead then, and I was living by myself in lodgings. Well, one day I got a letter from my intended, saying that she had seen me down at Southend on the Sunday, and that was enough for her. All was over between us.

"Now, it was most unfortunate that I'd had to put off seeing her that week-end, owing to an attack of influenza. It's a cruel thing to be ill all alone in lodgings, and nobody to look after you. You might die there all on your own and nobody the wiser. Just an unfurnished room I had, you see, and no attendance, and not a soul came near me, though I was pretty bad. But my young lady she said as she had seen me down at Southend with another young woman, and she would take no excuse. Of course, I said, what was *she* doing down at Southend without me, anyhow, and that tore it. She sent me back the ring, and the episode, as they say, was closed.

"But the thing that troubled me was, I was getting that shaky in my mind, how did I know I hadn't been to Southend without knowing it? I thought I'd been half sick and half asleep in my lodgings, but it was misty-like to me. And knowing the things I had done other times—well, there! I hadn't any clear recollection one way or another, except fever-dreams. I had a vague recollection of wandering and walking somewhere for hours together. Delirious, I thought I was, but it might have been sleep-walking for all I knew. I hadn't a leg to stand on by way of evidence. I felt it very hard, losing my intended like that, but I could have got over that if it hadn't been for the fear of myself and my brain giving way or something.

"You may think this is all foolishness and I was just being mixed up with some other fellow of the same name that happened to be very like me. But now I'll tell you something.

"Terrible dreams I got to having about that time. There was one thing as always haunted me—a thing that had frightened me as a little chap. My mother, though she was a good, strict woman, liked to go to a cinema now and again. Of course, in those days they weren't like what they are now, and I expect we should think those old pictures pretty crude if we was to see them, but we thought a lot of them at that time. When I

10

was about seven or eight I should think, she took me with her to see a thing—I remember the name now—*The Student of Prague*, it was called. I've forgotten the story, but it was a costume piece, about a young fellow at the university who sold himself to the devil, and one day his reflection came stalking out of the mirror on its own, and went about committing dreadful crimes, so that everybody thought it was him. At least, I think it was that, but I forget the details, it's so long ago. But what I shan't forget in a hurry is the fright it gave me to see that dretful figure come out of the mirror. It was that ghastly to see it, I cried and yelled, and after a time mother had to take me out. For months and years after that I used to dream of it. I'd dream I was looking in a great long glass, same as the student in the picture, and after a bit I'd see my reflection smiling at me and I'd walk up to the mirror holding out my left hand, it might be, and seeing myself walking to meet me with its right hand out. And just as it came up to me, it would suddenly—that was the awful moment—turn its back on me and walk away into the mirror again, grinning over its shoulder, and suddenly I'd know that *it* was the real person and *I* was only the reflection, and I'd make a dash after it into the mirror, and then everything would go grey and misty round me and with the horror of it I'd wake up all of a perspiration."

"Uncommonly disagreeable," said Wimsey. "That legend of the *Doppelgänger*, it's one of the oldest and the most widespread and never fails to terrify me. When *I* was a kid, my nurse had a trick that frightened me. If we'd been out, and she was asked if we'd met anybody, she used to say, 'Oh, no—we saw nobody nicer than ourselves.' I used to toddle after her in terror of coming round a corner and seeing a horrid and similar pair pouncing out at us. Of course I'd have rather died than tell a soul how the thing terrified me. Rum little beasts, kids."

The little man nodded thoughtfully.

"Well," he went on, "about that time the nightmare came back. At first it was only at intervals, you know, but it grew on me. At last it started coming every night. I hadn't hardly closed my eyes before there was the long mirror and the thing coming grinning along, always with its hand out as if it meant to catch hold of me and pull me through the glass. Sometimes I'd wake

11

up with the shock, but sometimes the dream went on, and I'd be stumbling for hours through a queer sort of world—all mist and half-lights, and the walls would be all crooked like they are in that picture of 'Dr. Caligari.' Lunatic, that's what it was. Many's the time I've sat up all night for fear of going to sleep. I didn't know, you see. I used to lock the bedroom door and hide the key for fear—you see, I didn't know what I might be doing. But then I read in a book that sleepwalkers can remember the places where they've hidden things when they were awake. So that was no use."

"Why didn't you get someone to share the room with you?"

"Well, I did." He hesitated. "I got a woman—she was a good kid. The dream went away then. I had blessed peace for three years. I was fond of that girl. Damned fond of her. Then she died."

He gulped down the last of his whiskey and blinked.

"Influenza, it was. Pneumonia. It kind of broke me up. Pretty she was, too. . . .

"After that, I was alone again. I felt bad about it. I couldn't— I didn't like—but the dreams came back. Worse. I dreamed about doing things—well! That doesn't matter now.

"And one day it came in broad daylight. . . .

"I was going along Holborn at lunch-time. I was still at Crichton's. Head of the packing department I was then, and doing pretty well. It was a wet beast of a day, I remember— dark and drizzling. I wanted a hair-cut. There's a barber shop on the south side, about half way along—one of those places where you go down a passage and there's a door at the end with a mirror and the name written across it in gold letters. You know what I mean.

"I went in there. There was a light in the passage, so I could see quite plainly. As I got up to the mirror I could see my reflection coming to meet me, and all of a sudden the awful dream-feeling came over me. I told myself it was all nonsense and put my hand out to the door-handle—my left hand, because the handle was that side and I was still apt to be left-handed when I didn't think about it.

"The reflection, of course, put out its right hand—that was all right, of course—and I saw my own figure in my old squash hat and burberry—but the face—oh, my god! It was grinning at me—and then just like in the dream, it suddenly turned its back and walked away from me, looking over its shoulder—

"I had my hand on the door, and it opened, and I felt myself stumbling and falling over the threshold.

"After that, I don't remember anything more. I woke up in my own bed and there was a doctor with me. He told me I had fainted in the street, and they'd found some letters on me with my address and taken me home.

"I told the doctor all about it, and he said I was in a highly nervous condition and ought to find a change of work and get out in the open air more.

"They were very decent to me at Crichton's. They put me on to inspecting their outdoor publicity. You know. One goes round from town to town inspecting the hoardings and seeing what posters are damaged or badly placed and reporting on them. They gave me a Morgan to run about in. I'm on that job now.

"The dreams are better. But I still have them. Only a few nights ago it came to me. One of the worst I've ever had. Fighting and strangling in a black, misty place. I'd tracked the devil—my other self—and got him down. I can feel my fingers on his throat now—killing myself.

"That was in London. I'm always worse in London. Then I came up here. . . .

"You see why that book interested me. The fourth dimension . . . it's not a thing I ever heard of, but this man Wells seems to know all about it. You're educated now. Daresay you've been to college and all that. What do you think about it, eh?"

"I should think, you know," said Wimsey, "it was more likely your doctor was right. Nerves and all that."

"Yes, but that doesn't account for me having got twisted round the way I am, now, does it? Legends, you talked of. Well, there's some people think those medeeval johnnies knew quite a lot. I don't say I believe in devils and all that. But maybe some of them may have been afflicted, same as me. It stands to reason they wouldn't talk such a lot about it if they

13

hadn't felt it, if you see what I mean., But what I'd like to know is, can't I get back any way? I tell you, it's a weight on my mind. I never know, you see."

"I shouldn't worry too much, if I were you," said Wimsey. "I'd stick to the fresh-air life. And I'd get married. Then you'd have a check on your movements, don't you see. And the dreams might go again."

"Yes. Yes. I've thought of that. But—did you read about that man the other day? Strangled his wife in his sleep, that's what he did. Now, supposing I—that would be a terrible thing to happen to a man, wouldn't it? Those dreams. . . ."

He shook his head and stared thoughtfully into the fire. Wimsey, after a short interval of silence, got up and went out into the bar. The landlady and the waiter and the barmaid were there, their heads close together over the evening paper. They were talking animatedly, but stopped abruptly at the sound of Wimsey's footsteps.

Ten minutes later, Wimsey returned to the lounge. The little man had gone. Taking up his motoring-coat, which he had flung on a chair, Wimsey went upstairs to his bedroom. He undressed slowly and thoughtfully, put on his pyjamas and dressing-gown, and then, pulling a copy of the *Evening News* from his motoring-coat pocket, he studied a front-page item attentively for some time. Presently he appeared to come to some decision, for he got up and opened his door cautiously. The passage was empty and dark. Wimsey switched on a torch and walked quietly along, watching the floor. Opposite one of the doors he stopped, contemplating a pair of shoes which stood waiting to be cleaned. Then he softly tried the door. It was locked. He tapped cautiously.,

A red head emerged.

"May I come in a moment?" said Wimsey, in a whisper.

The little man stepped back, and Wimsey followed him in.

"What's up?" said Mr. Duckworthy.

"I want to talk to you," said Wimsey. "Get back into bed, because it may take some time."

The little man looked at him, scared, but did as he was told. Wimsey gathered the folds of his dressing-gown closely about him, screwed his monocle more firmly into his eye, and sat down on the edge of the bed. He looked at Mr. Duckworthy a few minutes without speaking, and then said:

"Look here. You've told me a queerish story tonight. For some reason I believe you. Possibly it only shows what a silly ass I am, but I was born like that, so it's past praying for. Nice, trusting nature and so on. Have you seen the paper this evening?"

He pushed the *Evening News* into Mr. Duckworthy's hand and bent the monocle on him more glassily then ever.

On the front page was a photograph. Underneath was a panel in bold type, boxed for greater emphasis:

> The police at Scotland Yard are anxious to get into touch with the original of this photograph, which was found in the handbag of Miss Jessie Haynes, whose dead body was found strangled on Barnes Common last Thursday morning. The photograph bears on the back the words "J. H. with love from R. D." Anybody recognising the photograph is asked to communicate immediately with Scotland Yard or any police station.

Mr. Duckworthy looked, and grew so white that Wimsey thought he was going to faint.

"Well?" said Wimsey.

"Oh, God, sir! Oh, God! It's come at last." He whimpered and pushed the paper away, shuddering. "I've always known something of this would happen. But as sure as I'm born I knew nothing about it."

"It's you all right, I suppose?"

"The photograph's me all right. Though how it came there I *don't* know. I haven't had one taken for donkey's years, on my oath I haven't—except once in a staff group at Crichton's. But I tell you, sir, honest-to-God, there's times when I don't know what I'm doing, and that's a fact."

Wimsey examined the portrait feature by feature.

"Your nose, now—it has a slight twist—if you'll excuse my referring to it—to the right, and so it has in the photograph.

The left eyelid droops a little. That's correct, too. The forehead here seems to have a distinct bulge on the left side—unless that's an accident in the printing."

"No!" Mr. Duckworthy swept his tousled cowlick aside. "It's very conspicuous—unsightly, I always think, so I wear the hair over it."

With the ginger lock pushed back, his resemblance to the photograph was more startling than before.

"My mouth's crooked, too."

"So it is. Slants up to the left. Very attractive, a one-sided smile, I always think—on a face of your type, that is. I have known such things to look positively sinister."

Mr. Duckworthy smiled a faint, crooked smile.

"Do you know this girl, Jessie Haynes?"

"Not in my right senses, I don't, sir. Never heard of her—except, of course, that I read about the murder in the papers. Strangled—oh, my God!" He pushed his hands out in front of him and stared woefully at them.

"What can I do? If I was to get away—"

"You can't. They've recognised you down in the bar. The police will probably be here in a few minutes. No"—as Duckworthy made an attempt to get out of bed—"don't do that. It's no good, and it would only get you into worse trouble. Keep quiet and answer one or two questions. First of all, do you know who I am? No, how should you? My name's Wimsey—Lord Peter Wimsey—"

"The detective?"

"If you like to call it that. Now, listen. Where was it you lived at Brixton?"

The little man gave the address.

"You mother's dead. Any other relatives?"

"There was an aunt. She came from somewhere in Surrey, I think. Aunt Susan, I used to call her. I haven't seen her since I was a kid."

"Married?"

"Yes—oh, yes—Mrs. Susan Brown."

"Right. Were you left-handed as a child?"

"Well, yes, I was, at first. But mother broke me of it."

"And the tendency came back after the air-raid. And were you ever ill as a child? To have the doctor, I mean?"

"I had measles once, when I was about four."

"Remember the doctor's name?"

"They took me to the hospital."

"Oh, of course. Do you remember the name of the barber in Holborn?"

This question came so unexpectedly as to stagger the wits of Mr. Duckworthy, but after a while he said he thought it was Biggs or Briggs.

Wimsey sat thoughtfully for a moment, and then said:

"I think that's all. Except—oh, yes! What is your Christian name?"

"Robert."

"And you assure me that, so far as you know, you had no hand in this business?"

"That," said the little man, "that I swear to. As far as I know, you know. Oh, my Lord! If only it was possible to prove an alibi! That's my only chance. But I'm so afraid, you see, that I *may* have done it. Do you think—do you think they would hang me for that?"

"Not if you could prove you knew nothing about it," said Wimsey. He did not add that, even so, his acquaintance might probably pass the rest of his life at Broadmoor.

"And you know," said Mr. Duckworthy, "if I'm to go about all my life killing people without knowing it, it would be much better that they should hang me and done with it. It's a terrible thing to think of."

"Yes, but you may not have done it, you know."

"I hope not, I'm sure," said Mr. Duckworthy. "I say— what's that?"

"The police, I fancy," said Wimsey lightly. He stood up as a knock came at the door, and said heartily, "Come in!"

The landlord, who entered first, seemed rather taken aback by Wimsey's presence.

"Come right in," said Wimsey hospitably. "Come in, sergeant; come in, officer. What can we do for you?"

"Don't," said the landlord, "don't make a row if you can help it."

17

The police sergeant paid no attention to either of them, but stalked across to the bed and confronted the shrinking Mr. Duckworthy.

"It's the man all right," said he. "Now, Mr. Duckworthy, you'll excuse this late visit, but as you may have seen by the papers, we've been looking for a person answering your description, and there's no time like the present. We want—"

"I didn't do it," cried Mr. Duckworthy wildly. "I know nothing about it—"

The officer pulled out his note-book and wrote: "He said before any question was asked him, 'I didn't do it.'"

"You seem to know all about it," said the sergeant.

"Of course he does," said Wimsey; "we've been having a little informal chat about it."

"You have, have you? And who might you be—sir?" The last word appeared to be screwed out of the sergeant forcibly by the action of the monocle.

"I'm so sorry," said Wimsey, "I haven't a card on me at the moment. I am Lord Peter Wimsey."

"Oh, indeed," said the sergeant. "And may I ask, my lord, what you know about this here?"

"You may, and I may answer if I like, you know. I know nothing at all about the murder. About Mr. Duckworthy I know what he was told me and no more. I dare say he will tell you, too, if you ask him nicely. But no third degree, you know, sergeant. No Savidgery."

Baulked by this painful reminder, the sergeant said, in a voice of annoyance:

"It's my duty to ask him what he knows about this."

"I quite agree," said Wimsey. "As a good citizen, it's his duty to answer you. But it's a gloomy time of night, don't you think? Why not wait till the morning? Mr. Duckworthy won't run away."

"I'm not so sure of that."

"Oh, but I am. I will undertake to produce him whenever you want him. Won't that do? You're not charging him with anything, I suppose?"

"Not yet," said the sergeant.

"Splendid. Then it's all quite friendly and pleasant, isn't it? How about a drink?"

The sergeant refused this kindly offer with some gruffness in his manner.

"On the waggon?" inquired Wimsey sympathetically. "Bad luck. Kidneys? Or liver, eh?"

The sergeant made no reply.

"Well, we are charmed to have had the pleasure of seeing you," pursued Wimsey. "You'll look us up in the morning, won't you? I've got to get back to town fairly early, but I'll drop in at the police-station on my way. You will find Mr. Duckworthy in the lounge, here. It will be more comfortable for you than at your place. Must you be going? Well, good night, all."

Later, Wimsey returned to Mr. Duckworthy, after seeing the police off the premises.

"Listen," he said, "I'm going up to town to do what I can. I'll send you up a solicitor first thing in the morning. Tell him what you've told me, and tell the police what he tells you to tell them and no more. Remember, they can't force you to say anything or to go down to the police-station unless they charge you. If they do charge you, go quietly and say nothing. And whatever you do, don't run away, because if you do, you're done for."

Wimsey arrived in town the following afternoon, and walked down Holborn, looking for a barber's shop. He found it without much difficulty. It lay, as Mr. Duckworthy had described it, at the end of a narrow passage, and it had a long mirror in the door, with the name Briggs scrawled across it in gold letters. Wimsey stared at his own reflection distastefully.

"Check number one," said he, mechanically setting his tie to rights. "Have I been led up the garden? Or is it a case of fourth dimensional mystery? 'The animals went in four by four, *vive la compagnie!* The camel he got stuck in the door.' There is something intensely unpleasant about making a camel of one's self. It goes for days without a drink and its table-manners are objectionable. But there is no doubt that this door is made of looking-glass. Was it always so, I wonder? On, Wimsey, on. I cannot bear to be shaved again. Perhaps a hair-cut might be managed."

He pushed the door open, keeping a stern eye on his reflection to see that it played him no trick.

Of his conversation with the barber, which was lively and varied, only one passage is deserving of record.

"It's some time since I was in here," said Wimsey. "Keep it short behind the ears. Been re-decorated, haven't you?"

"Yes, sir. Looks quite smart, doesn't it?"

"The mirror on the outside of the door—that's new, too, isn't it?"

"Oh, no, sir. That's been there ever since we took over."

"Has it! Then it's longer ago than I thought. Was it there three years ago?"

"Oh, yes, sir. Ten years Mr. Briggs has been here, sir."

"And the mirror, too?"

"Oh, yes, sir."

"Then it's my memory that's wrong. Senile decay setting in. 'All, all are gone, the old familiar landmarks.' No, thanks, if I go grey I'll go grey decently. I don't want any hair-tonics to-day, thank you. No, nor even an electric comb. I've had shocks enough."

It worried him, though. So much so that when he emerged, he walked back a few yards along the street, and was suddenly struck by seeing the glass door of a tea-shop. It also lay at the end of a dark passage and had a gold name written across it. The name was "The BRIDGET Tea-shop," but the door was of plain glass. Wimsey looked at it for a few moments and then went in. He did not approach the tea-tables, but accosted the cashier, who sat at a little glass desk inside the door.

Here he went straight to the point and asked whether the young lady remembered the circumstance of a man's having fainted in the doorway some years previously.

The cashier could not say; she had only been there three months, but she thought one of the waitresses might remember. The waitress was produced, and after some consideration, thought she did recollect something of the sort. Wimsey thanked her, said he was a journalist—which seemed to be accepted

20

as an excuse for eccentric questions—parted with half a crown, and withdrew.

His next visit was to Carmelite House. Wimsey had friends in every newspaper office in Fleet Street, and made his way without difficulty to the room where photographs are filed for reference. The original of the "J.D." portrait was produced for his inspection.

"One of yours?" he asked.

"Oh, no. Sent out by Scotland Yard. Why? Anything wrong with it?"

"Nothing. I wanted the name of the original photographer, that's all."

"Oh! Well, you'll have to ask them there. Nothing more I can do for you?"

"Nothing, thanks."

Scotland Yard was easy. Chief-Inspector Parker was Wimsey's closest friend. An inquiry of him soon furnished the photographer's name, which was inscribed at the foot of the print. Wimsey voyaged off at once in search of the establishment, where his name readily secured an interview with the proprietor.

As he had expected, Scotland Yard had been there before him. All information at the disposal of the firm had already been given. It amounted to very little. The photograph had been taken a couple of years previously, and nothing particular was remembered about the sitter. It was a small establishment, doing a rapid business in cheap portraits, and with no pretensions to artistic refinements.

Wimsey asked to see the original negative, which, after some search, was produced.

Wimsey looked it over, laid it down, and pulled from his pocket the copy of the *Evening News* in which the print had appeared.

"Look at this," he said.

The proprietor looked, then looked back at the negative.

"Well, I'm dashed," he said. "That's funny."

"It was done in the enlarging lantern, I take it," said Wimsey.

"Yes. It must have been put in the wrong way round. Now,

21

fancy that happening. You know, sir, we often have to work against time, and I suppose—but it's very careless. I shall have to inquire into it."

"Get me a print of it right way round," said Wimsey.

"Yes, sir, certainly, sir. At once."

"And send one to Scotland Yard."

"Yes, sir. Queer it should have been just this particular one, isn't it, sir? I wonder the party didn't notice. But we generally take three or four positions, and he might not remember, you know."

"You'd better see if you've got any other positions and let me have them too."

"I've done that already, sir, but there are none. No doubt this one was selected and the others destroyed. We don't keep all the rejected negatives, you know, sir. We haven't the space to file them. But I'll get three prints off at once."

"Do," said Wimsey. "The sooner the better. Quick-dry them. And don't do any work on the prints."

"No, sir. You shall have them in an hour or two, sir. But it's astonishing to me that the party didn't complain."

"It's not astonishing," said Wimsey. "He probably thought it the best likeness of the lot. And so it would be—to him. Don't you see—that's the only view he could ever take of his own face. That photograph, with the left and right sides reversed, is the face he sees in the mirror every day—the only face he can really recognise as his. 'Wad the gods the giftie gie us,' and all that."

"Well, that's quite true, sir. And I'm much obliged to you for pointing the mistake out."

Wimsey reiterated the need for haste, and departed. A brief visit to Somerset House followed; after which he called it a day and went home.

Inquiry in Brixton, in and about the address mentioned by Mr. Duckworthy, eventually put Wimsey on to the track of persons who had known him and his mother. An aged lady who had kept a small green-grocery in the same street for the last forty years remembered all about them. She had the en-

22

cyclopaedic memory of the almost illiterate, and was positive as to the date of their arrival.

"Thirty-two years ago, if we lives another month," she said. "Michaelmas it was they come. She was a nice-looking young woman, too, and my daughter, as was expecting her first, took a lot of interest in the sweet little boy."

"The boy was not born here?"

"Why, no, sir. Born somewheres on the south side, he was, but I remember she never rightly said where—only that it was round about the New Cut. She was one of the quiet sort and kep' herself to herself. Never one to talk, she wasn't. Why even to my daughter, as might 'ave good reason for bein' interested, she wouldn't say much about 'ow she got through 'er bad time. Chlorryform she said she 'ad, I know, and she disremembered about it, bit it's my belief it 'ad gone 'ard with 'er and she didn't care to think overmuch about it. 'Er 'usband—a nice man 'e was, too—'e says to me, 'Don't remind 'er of it, Mrs. 'Arbottle, don't remind 'er of it.' Whether she was frightened or whether she was 'urt by it I don't know, but she didn't 'ave no more children. 'Lor!' I says to 'er time and again, 'you'll get used to it, my dear, when you've 'ad nine of 'em same as me,' and she smiled, but she never 'ad no more, none the more for that."

"I suppose it does take some getting used to," said Wimsey, "but nine of them don't seem to have hurt *you*, Mrs. Harbottle, if I may say so. You look extremely flourishing."

"I keeps my 'ealth, sir. I am glad to say, though stouter than I used to be. Nine of them does 'ave a kind of spreading action on the figure. You wouldn't believe, sir, to look at me now, as I 'ad a eighteen-inch waist when I was a girl. Many's the time me pore mother broke the laces on me, with 'er knee in me back and me 'oldin' on the bedpost."

"One must suffer to be beautiful," said Wimsey politely. "How old was the baby, then, when Mrs. Duckworthy came to live in Brixton?"

"Three weeks old, 'e was, sir—a darling dear—and a lot of 'air on 'is 'ead. Black 'air it was then, but it turned into the brightest red you ever see—like them carrots there. It wasn't so pretty as 'is ma's, though much the same colour. He didn't

23

favour 'er in the face, neither, nor yet 'is dad. She said 'e took after some of 'er side of the family."

"Did you ever see any of the rest of the family?"

"Only 'er sister, Mrs. Susan Brown. A big, stern, 'ard-faced woman she was—not like 'er sister. Lived at Evesham she did, as well I remembers, for I was gettin' my grass from there at the time. I never sees a bunch o' grass now but what I think of Mrs. Susan Brown. Stiff, she was, with a small 'ead, very like a stick o' grass."

Wimsey thanked Mrs. Harbottle in a suitable manner and took the next train to Evesham. He was beginning to wonder where the chase might lead him, but discovered, much to his relief, that Mrs. Susan Brown was well known in the town, being a pillar of the Methodist Chapel and a person well respected. She was upright still, with smooth, dark hair parted in the middle and drawn tightly back—a woman broad in the base and narrow in the shoulder—not, indeed, unlike the stick of asparagus to which Mrs. Harbottle had compared her. She received Wimsey with stern civility, but disclaimed all knowledge of her nephew's movements. The hint that he was in a position of some embarrassment, and even danger, did not appear to surprise her.

"There was bad blood in him," she said. "My sister Hetty was softer by half than she ought to have been."

"Ah!" said Wimsey. "Well, we can't all be people of strong character, though it must be a source of great satisfaction to those that are. I don't want to be a trouble to you, madam, and I know I'm given to twaddling rather, being a trifle on the soft side myself—so I'll get to the point. I see by the register at Somerset House that your nephew, Robert Duckworthy, was born in Southwark, the son of Alfred and Hester Duckworthy. Wonderful system they have there. But of course—being only human—it breaks down now and again—doesn't it?"

She folded her wrinkled hands over one another on the edge of the table, and he saw a kind of shadow flicker over her sharp dark eyes.

"If I'm not bothering you too much—in what name was the other registered?"

The hands trembled a little, but she said steadily:

"I do not understand you."

"I'm frightfully sorry. Never was good at explaining myself. There were twin boys born, weren't there? Under what name did they register the other? I'm so sorry to be a nuisance, but it's really rather important."

"What makes you suppose that there were twins?"

"Oh, I don't suppose it. I wouldn't have bothered you for a supposition. I know there was a twin brother. What became— at least, I do know more or less what became of him—"

"It died," she said hurriedly.

"I hate to seem contradictory," said Wimsey. "Most unattractive behaviour. But it didn't die, you know. In fact, it's alive now. It's only the name I want to know, you know."

"And why should I tell you anything, young man?"

"Because," said Wimsey, "if you will pardon the mention of anything so disagreeable to a refined taste, there's been a murder committed and your nephew Robert is suspected. As a matter of fact, I happen to know that the murder was done by the brother. That's why I want to get hold of him, don't you see. It would be such a relief to my mind—I am naturally nice-minded—if you would help me to find him. Because, if not, I shall have to go to the police, and then you might be subpoena'd as a witness, and I shouldn't like—I really shouldn't like—to see you in the witness-box at a murder trial. So much unpleasant publicity, don't you know. Whereas, if we can lay hands on the brother quickly, you and Robert need never come into it at all."

Mrs. Brown sat in grim thought for a few minutes.

"Very well, she said, "I will tell you."

"Of course," said Wimsey to Chief-Inspector Parker a few days later, "the whole thing was quite obvious when one had heard about the reversal of friend Duckworthy's interior economy."

"No doubt, no doubt," said Parker. "Nothing could be simpler. But all the same, you are aching to tell me how you deduced it and I am willing to be instructed. Are all twins wrong-sided? And are all wrong-sided people twins?"

"Yes. No. Or rather, no, yes. Dissimilar twins and some kinds of similar twins may both be quite normal. But the kind of similar twins that result from the splitting of a single cell *may* come out as looking-glass twins. It depends on the line of fission in the original cell. You can do it artificially with tadpoles and a bit of horsehair."

"I will make a note to do it at once," said Parker gravely.

"In fact, I've read somewhere that a person with a reversed inside practically always turns out to be one of a pair of similar twins. So you see, while poor old R. D. was burbling on about the *Student of Prague* and the fourth dimension, I was expecting the twin-brother.

"Apparently what happened was this. There were three sisters of the name of Dart—Susan, Hester and Emily. Susan married a man called Brown; Hester married a man called Duckworthy; Emily was unmarried. By one of those cheery little ironies of which life is so full, the only sister who had a baby, or who was apparently capable of having babies, was the unmarried Emily. By way of compensation, she overdid it and had twins.

"When this catastrophe was about to occur, Emily (deserted, of course, by the father) confided in her sisters, the parents being dead. Susan was a tartar—besides, she had married above her station and was climbing steadily on a ladder of good works. She delivered herself of a few texts and washed her hands of the business. Hester was a kind-hearted soul. She offered to adopt the infant, when produced, and bring it up as her own. Well, the baby came, and, as I said before, it was twins.

"That was a bit too much for Duckworthy. He had agreed to one baby, but twins were more than he had bargained for. Hester was allowed to pick her twin, and, being a kindly soul, she picked the weaklier-looking one, which was our Robert— the mirror-image twin. Emily had to keep the other, and, as soon as she was strong enough, decamped with him to Australia, after which she was no more heard of.

"Emily's twin was registered in her own name of Dart and baptised Richard. Robert and Richard were two pretty men. Robert was registered as Hester Duckworthy's own child—there were no tiresome rules in those days requiring notification of births by doctors and midwives, so one could do as one liked about these matters. The Duckworthys, complete with baby, moved to Brixton, where Robert was looked upon as being a perfectly genuine little Duckworthy.

"Apparently Emily died in Australia, and Richard, then a boy of fifteen, worked his passage home to London. He does not seem to have been a nice little boy. Two years afterwards, his path crossed that of Brother Robert and produced the episode of the air-raid night.

"Hester may have known about the wrong-sidedness of Robert, or she may not. Anyway, he wasn't told. I imagine that the shock of the explosion caused him to revert more strongly to his natural left-handed tendency. It also seems to have induced a new tendency to amnesia under similar shock-conditions. The whole thing preyed on his mind, and he became more and more vague and somnambulant.

"I rather think that Richard may have discovered the existence of his double and turned it to account. That explains the central incident of the mirror. I think Robert must have mistaken the glass door of the teashop for the door of the barber's shop. It really was Richard who came to meet him, and who retired again so hurriedly for fear of being seen and noted. Circumstances played into his hands, of course—but these meetings do take place, and the fact that they were both wearing soft hats and burberries is not astonishing on a dark, wet day.

"And then there is the photograph. No doubt the original mistake was the photographer's, but I shouldn't be surprised if Richard welcomed it and chose that particular print on that account. Though that would mean, of course, that he knew about the wrong-sidedness of Robert. I don't know how he could have done that, but he may have had opportunities for inquiry. It was known in the Army, and the rumours may have got round. But I won't press that point.

"There's one rather queer thing, and that is that Robert should have had that dream about strangling, on the very night, as far as one could make out, that Richard was engaged in doing away with Jessie Haynes. They say that similar twins are always in close sympathy with one another—that each knows

27

what the other is thinking about, for instance, and contracts the same illness on the same day and all that. Richard was the stronger twin of the two, and perhaps he dominated Robert more than Robert did him. I'm sure I don't know. Daresay it's all bosh. The point is that you've found him all right."

"Yes. Once we'd got the clue there was no difficulty."

"Well, let's toddle round to the Cri and have one."

Wimsey got up and set his tie to rights before the glass.

"All the same," he said, "there's something queer about mirrors. Uncanny, a bit, don't you think so?"

CHAPTER II

◆

The Incredible Elopement of Lord Peter Wimsey

"THAT house, señor?" said the landlord of the little *posada*. "That is the house of the American physician, whose wife, may the blessed saints preserve us, is bewitched." He crossed himself, and so did his wife and daughter.

"Bewitched, is she?" said Langley sympathetically. He was a professor of ethnology, and this was not his first visit to the Pyrenees. He had, however, never before penetrated to any place quite so remote as this tiny hamlet, clinging, like a rock-plant, high up the scarred granite shoulders of the mountain. He scented material here for his book on Basque folk-lore. With tact, he might persuade the old man to tell his story.

"And in what manner," he asked, "is the lady be-spelled?"

"Who knows?" replied the landlord, shrugging his shoulders. "'The man that asked questions on Friday was buried on Saturday.' Will your honour consent to take his supper?"

Langley took the hint. To press the question would be to encounter obstinate silence. Later, when they knew him better, perhaps—

His dinner was served to him at the family table—the

oily, pepper-flavoured stew to which he was so well accustomed, and the harsh red wine of the country. His hosts chattered to him freely enough in that strange Basque language which has no fellow in the world, and is said by some to be the very speech of our first fathers in Paradise. They spoke of the bad winter, and young Esteban Arramandy, so strong and swift at the pelota, who had been lamed by a falling rock and now halted on two sticks; of three valuable goats carried off by a bear; of the torrential rains that, after a dry summer, had scoured the bare ribs of the mountains. It was raining now, and the wind was howling unpleasantly. This did not trouble Langley; he knew and loved this haunted and impenetrable country at all times and seasons. Sitting in that rude peasant inn, he thought of the oak-panelled hall of his Cambridge college and smiled, and his eyes gleamed happily behind his scholarly pince-nez. He was a young man, in spite of his professorship and the string of letters after his name. To his university colleagues it seemed strange that this man, so trim, so prim, so early old, should spend his vacations eating garlic, and scrambling on mule-back along precipitous mountain-tracks. You would never think it, they said, to look at him.

There was a knock at the door.

"That is Martha," said the wife.

She drew back the latch, letting in a rush of wind and rain which made the candle gutter. A small, aged woman was blown in out of the night, her grey hair straggling in wisps from beneath her shawl.

"Come in, Martha, and rest yourself. It is a bad night. The parcel is ready—oh, yes. Dominique brought it from the town this morning. You must take a cup of wine or milk before you go back."

The old woman thanked her and sat down, panting.

"And how goes all at the house? The doctor is well?"

"He is well."

"And *she?*"

The daughter put the question in a whisper, and the landlord shook his head at her with a frown.

"As always at this time of the year. It is but a month now

29

to the Day of the Dead. Jesu-Maria! It is a grievous affliction for the poor gentleman, but he is patient, patient."

"He is a good man," said Dominique, "and a skillful doctor, but an evil like that is beyond his power to cure. You are not afraid, Martha?"

"Why should I be afraid? The Evil One cannot harm *me*. I have no beauty, no wits, no strength for him to envy. And the Holy Relic will protect me."

Her wrinkled fingers touched something in the bosom of her dress.

"You come from the house yonder?" asked Langley.

She eyed him suspiciously.

"The señor is not of our country?"

"The gentleman is a guest, Martha," said the landlord hurriedly. "A learned English gentleman. He knows our country and speaks our language as you hear. He is a great traveller, like the American doctor, your master."

"What is your master's name?" asked Langley. It occurred to him that an American doctor who had buried himself in this remote corner of Europe must have something unusual about him. Perhaps he also was an ethnologist. If so, they might find something in common."

"He is called Wetherall." She pronounced the name several times before he was sure of it?"

"Wetherall? Not Standish Wetherall?"

He was filled with extraordinary excitement.

The landlord came to his assistance.

"This parcel is for him," he said. "No doubt the name will be written there."

It was a small package, neatly sealed, bearing the label of a firm of London chemists and addressed to "Standish Wetherall, Esq., M.D."

"Good heavens!" exclaimed Langley. "But this is strange. Almost a miracle. I know this man. I knew his wife, too—"

He stopped. Again the company made the sign of the cross.

"Tell me," he said in great agitation, and forgetting his caution, "you say his wife is bewitched—afflicted—how is this? Is she the same woman I know? Describe her. She was

30

tall, beautiful, with gold hair and blue eyes like the Madonna.
Is this she?"

There was a silence. The old woman shook her head and
muttered something inaudible, but the daughter whispered:

"True—it is true. Once we saw her thus, as the gentleman
says—"

"Be quiet," said her father.

"Sir," said Martha, "we are in the hands of God."

She rose, and wrapped her shawl about her.

"One moment," said Langley. He pulled out his notebook
and scribbled a few lines. "Will you take this letter to your
master the doctor? It is to say that I am here, his friend whom
he once knew, and to ask if I may come and visit him. That
is all."

"You would not go to that house, excellence?" whispered
the old woman fearfully.

"If he will not have me, maybe he will come to me here."
He added a word or two and drew a piece of money from his
pocket. "You will carry my note for me?"

"Willingly, willingly. But the señor will be careful? Perhaps, though a foreigner, you are of the Faith?"

"I am a Christian," said Langley.

This seemed to satisfy her. She took the letter and the
money, and secured them, together with the parcel, in a remote
pocket. Then she walked to the door, strongly and rapidly for
all her bent shoulders and appearance of great age.

Langley remained lost in thought. Nothing could have
astonished him more than to meet the name of Standish Wetherall in this place. He had thought that episode finished and
done with over three years ago. Of all people! The brilliant
surgeon in the prime of his life and reputation, and Alice
Wetherall, that delicate piece of golden womanhood—exiled
in this forlorn corner of the world! His heart beat a little faster
at the thought of seeing her again. Three years ago, he had
decided that it would be wiser if he did not see too much of
that porcelain loveliness. That folly was past now—but still
he could not visualize her except against the background of
the great white house in Riverside Drive, with the peacocks
and the swimming-pool and the gilded tower with the roof-

garden. Wetherall was a rich man, the son of old Hiram Wetherall the automobile magnate. What was Wetherall doing here?

He tried to remember. Hiram Wetherall, he knew, was dead, and all the money belonged to Standish, for there were no other children. There had been trouble when the only son had married a girl without parents or history. He had brought her from "somewhere out west." There had been some story of his having found her, years before, as a neglected orphan, and saved her from something or cured her of something and paid for her education, when he was still scarcely more than a student. Then, when he was a man over forty and she a girl of seventeen, he had brought her home and married her.

And now he had left his house and his money and one of the finest specialist practices in New York to come to live in the Basque country—in a spot so out of the way that men still believed in Black Magic, and could barely splutter more than a few words of bastard French or Spanish—a spot that was uncivilised even by comparison with the primitive civilisation surrounding it. Langley began to be sorry that he had written to Wetherall. It might be resented.

The landlord and his wife had gone out to see to their cattle. The daughter sat close to the fire, mending a garment. She did not look at him, but he had the feeling that she would be glad to speak.

"Tell me, child," he said gently, "what is the trouble which afflicts these people who may be friends of mine?"

"Oh!" She glanced up quickly and leaned across to him, her arms stretched out over the sewing in her lap. "Sir, be advised. Do not go up there. No one will stay in that house at this time of the year, except Tomaso, who has not all his wits, and old Martha, who is—"

"What?"

"A saint—or something else," she said hurriedly.

"Child," said Langley again, "this lady when I knew—"

"I will tell you," she said, "but my father must not know. The good doctor brought her here three years ago last June, and then she was as you say. She was beautiful. She laughed and talked in her own speech—for she knew no Spanish or Basque. But on the Night of the Dead—"

32

She crossed herself.

"All-Hallows Eve," said Langley softly.

"Indeed, I do not know what happened. But she fell into the power of the darkness. She changed. There were terrible cries—I cannot tell. But little by little she became what she is now. Nobody sees her but Martha and she will not talk. But the people say it is not a woman at all that lives there now."

"Mad?" said Langley.

"It is not madness. It is—enchantment. Listen. Two years since on Easter Day—is that my father?"

"No, no."

"The sun had shone and the wind came up from the valley. We heard the blessed church bells all day long. That night there came a knock at the door. My father opened and one stood there like Our Blessed Lady herself, very pale like the image in the church and with a blue cloak over her head. She spoke, but we could not tell what she said. She wept and wrung her hands and pointed down the valley path, and my father went to the stable and saddled the mule. I thought of the flight from bad King Herod. But then—the American doctor came. He had run fast and was out of breath. And she shrieked at the sight of him."

A great wave of indignation swept over Langley. If the man was brutal to his wife, something must be done quickly. The girl hurried on.

"He said—Jesu-Maria—he said that his wife was bewitched. At Easter-tide the power of the Evil One was broken and she would try to flee. But as soon as the Holy Season was over, the spell would fall on her again, and therefore it was not safe to let her go. My parents were afraid to have touched the evil thing. They brought out the Holy Water and sprinkled the mule, but the wickedness had entered into the poor beast and she kicked my father so that he was lame for a month. The American took his wife away with him and we never saw her again. Even old Martha does not always see her. But every year the power waxes and wanes—heaviest at Hallow-tide and lifted again at Easter. Do not go to that house, senōr, if you value your soul! Hush! They are coming back."

Langley would have liked to ask more, but his host glanced

33

quickly and suspiciously at the girl. Taking up his candle, Langley went to bed. He dreamed of wolves, long, lean and black, running on the scent of blood.

Next day brought an answer to his letter:

DEAR LANGLEY,—Yes, this is myself, and of course I remember you well. Only too delighted to have you come and cheer our exile. You will find Alice somewhat changed, I fear, but I will explain our misfortunes when we meet. Our household is limited, owing to some kind of superstitious avoidance of the afflicted, but if you will come along about half-past seven, we can give you a meal of sorts. Martha will show you the way.

Cordially

STANDISH WETHERALL.

The doctor's house was small and old, stuck halfway up the mountainside on a kind of ledge in the rock-wall. A stream, unseen but clamorous, fell echoing down close at hand. Langley followed his guide into a dim, square room with a great hearth at one end and, drawn close before the fire, an armchair with wide, sheltering ears. Martha, muttering some sort of apology, hobbled away and left him standing there in the half-light. The flames of the wood fire, leaping and falling, made here a gleam and there a gleam, and, as his eyes grew familiar with the room, he saw that in the centre was a table laid for a meal, and that there were pictures on the walls. One of these struck a familiar note. He went close to it and recognised a portrait of Alice Wetherall that he had last seen in New York. It was painted by Sargent in his happiest mood, and the lovely wild-flower face seemed to lean down to him with the sparkling smile of life.

A log suddenly broke and fell to the hearth, flaring. As though the little noise and light had disturbed something, he heard, or thought he heard, a movement from the big chair before the fire. He stepped forward, and then stopped. There was nothing to be seen, but a noise had begun; a kind of low, animal muttering, extremely disagreeable to listen to. It was not made by a dog or a cat, he felt sure. It was a sucking, slobbering sound that affected him in a curiously sickening way. It ended in series of little grunts or squeals, and then there was silence.

Langley stepped backwards toward the door. He was positive that something was in the room with him that he did not care about meeting. An absurd impulse seized him to run away. He was prevented by the arrival of Martha, carrying a big, old-fashioned lamp, and behind her Wetherall, who greeted him cheerfully.

The familiar American accents dispelled the atmosphere of discomfort that had been gathering about Langley. He held out a cordial hand.

"Fancy meeting *you* here," said he.

"The world is very small," replied Wetherall. "I am afraid that is a hardy bromide, but I certainly am pleased to see you," he added, with some emphasis.

The old woman had put the lamp on the table, and now asked if she should bring in the dinner. Wetherall replied in the affirmative, using a mixture of Spanish and Basque which she seemed to understand well enough.

"I didn't know you were a Basque scholar," said Langley.

"Oh, one picks it up. These people speak nothing else. But of course Basque is your specialty, isn't it?"

"Oh, yes."

"I daresay they have told you some queer things about us. But we'll go into that later. I've managed to make the place reasonably comfortable, though I could do with a few more modern conveniences. However, it suits us."

Langley took the opportunity to mumble some sort of inquiry about Mrs. Wetherall.

"Alice? Ah, yes, I forgot—you have not seen her yet." Wetherall looked hard at him with a kind of half-smile. "I should have warned you. You were—rather an admirer of my wife in the old days."

"Like everyone else," said Langley.

"No doubt. Nothing specially surprising about it, was there? Here comes dinner. Put it down, Martha, and we will ring when we are ready."

The old woman set down a dish upon the table, which

was handsomely furnished with glass and silver, and went out. Wetherall moved over to the fireplace, stepping sideways and keeping his eyes oddly fixed on Langley. Then he addressed the armchair.

"Alice! Get up, my dear, and welcome an old admirer of yours. Come along. You will both enjoy it. Get up."

Something shuffled and whimpered among the cushions. Wetherall stooped, with an air of almost exaggerated courtesy, and lifted it to its feet. A moment, and it faced Langley in the lamplight.

It was dressed in a rich gown of gold satin and lace, that hung rucked and crumpled upon the thick and slouching body. The face was white and puffy, the eyes vacant, the mouth drooled open, with little trickles of saliva running from the loose corners. A dry fringe of rusty hair clung to the half-bald scalp, like the dead wisps on the head of a mummy.

"Come, my love," said Wetherall. "Say how do you do to Mr. Langley."

The creature blinked and mouthed out some inhuman sounds. Wetherall put his hand under its forearm, and it slowly extended a lifeless paw.

"There, she recognises you all right. I thought she would. Shake hands with him, my dear."

With a sensation of nausea, Langley took the inert hand. It was clammy and coarse to the touch and made no attempt to return his pressure. He let it go; it pawed vaguely in the air for a moment and then dropped.

"I was afraid you might be upset," said Wetherall, watching him. "I have grown used to it, of course, and it doesn't affect me as it would an outsider. Not that you are an outsider— anything but that—eh? Premature senility is the lay name for it, I suppose. Shocking, of course, if you haven't met it before. You needn't mind, by the way, what you say. She understands nothing."

"How did it happen?"

"I don't quite know. Came on gradually. I took the best advice, naturally, but there was nothing to be done. So we came here. I didn't care about facing things at home where everybody knew us. And I didn't like the idea of a sanatorium.

Alice is my wife, you know—sickness or health, for better, for worse, and all that. Come along; dinner's getting cold."

He advanced to the table, leading his wife, whose dim eyes seemed to brighten a little at the sight of food.

"Sit down, my dear, and eat your nice dinner. (She understands that, you see.) You'll excuse her table manners, won't you? They're not pretty, but you'll get used to them."

He tied a napkin round the neck of the creature and placed food before her in a deep bowl. She snatched at it hungrily, slavering and gobbling as she scooped it up in her fingers and smeared face and hands with the gravy.

Wetherall drew out a chair for his guest opposite to where his wife sat. The sight of her held Langley with a kind of disgusted fascination.

The food—a sort of salmis—was deliciously cooked, but Langley had no appetite. The whole thing was an outrage, to the pitiful woman and to himself. Her seat was directly beneath the Sargent portrait, and his eyes went helplessly from the one to the other.

"Yes," said Wetherall, following his glance. "There is a difference, isn't there?" He himself was eating heartily and apparently enjoying his dinner. "Nature plays sad tricks upon us."

"Is it always like this?"

"No; this is one of her bad days. At times she will be— almost human. Of course these people here don't know what to think of it all. They have their own explanation of a very simple medical phenomenon."

"Is there any hope of recovery?"

"I'm afraid not—not of a permanent cure. You are not eating anything."

"I—well, Wetherall, this has been a shock to me."

"Of course. Try a glass of burgundy. I ought not to have asked you to come, but the idea of talking to an educated fellow-creature once again tempted me. I must confess."

"It must be terrible for you."

"I have become resigned. Ah, naughty, naughty!" The idiot had flung half the contents of her bowl upon the table. Wetherall patiently remedied the disaster, and went on:

"I can bear it better here, in this wild place where everything seems possible and nothing unnatural. My people are all dead, so there was nothing to prevent me from doing as I liked about it."

"No. What about your property in the States?"

"Oh, I run over from time to time to keep an eye on things. In fact, I am due to sail next month. I'm glad you caught me. Nobody over there knows how we're fixed, of course. They just know we're living in Europe."

"Did you consult no American doctor?"

"No. We were in Paris when the first symptoms declared themselves. That was shortly after that visit you paid to us." A flash of some emotion to which Langley could not put a name made the doctor's eyes for a moment sinister. "The best men on this side confirmed my own diagnosis. So we came here."

He rang for Martha, who removed the salmis and put on a kind of sweet pudding.

"Martha is my right hand," observed Wetherall. "I don't know what we shall do without her. When I am away, she looks after Alice like a mother. Not that there's much one can do for her, except to keep her fed and warm and clean—and the last is something of a task."

There was a note in his voice which jarred on Langley. Wetherall noticed his recoil and said:

"I won't disguise from you that it gets on my nerves sometimes. But it can't be helped. Tell me about yourself. What have you been doing lately?"

Langley replied with as much vivacity as he could assume, and they talked of indifferent subjects till the deplorable being which had once been Alice Wetherall began to mumble and whine fretfully and scramble down from her chair.

"She's cold," said Wetherall. "Go back to the fire, my dear."

He propelled her briskly towards the hearth, and she sank back into the armchair, crouching and complaining and thrusting out her hands toward the blaze. Wetherall brought out brandy and a box of cigars.

"I contrive just to keep in touch with the world, you see," he said. "They send me these from London. And I get the latest medical journals and reports. I'm writing a book, you know, on my own subject; so I don't vegetate. I can experiment, too—plenty of room for a laboratory, and no Vivisection Acts to bother one. It's a good country to work in. Are you staying here long?"

"I think not very."

"Oh! If you had thought of stopping on, I would have offered you the use of this house while I was away. You would find it more comfortable than the *posada*, and I should have no qualms, you know, about leaving you alone in the place with my wife—under the peculiar circumstances."

He stressed the last words and laughed. Langley hardly knew what to say.

"Really, Wetherall—"

"Though, in the old days, *you* might have liked the prospect more and *I* might have liked it less. There was a time, I think, Langley, when you would have jumped at the idea of being alone with—*my wife.*"

Langley jumped up.

"What the devil are you insinuating, Wetherall?"

"Nothing, nothing. I was just thinking of the afternoon when you and she wandered away at a picnic and got lost. You remember? Yes, I thought you would."

"This is monstrous," retorted Langley. "How dare you say such things—with that poor soul sitting there—?"

"Yes, poor soul. You're a poor thing to look at now, aren't you, my kitten?"

He turned suddenly to the woman. Something in his abrupt gesture seemed to frighten her, and she shrank away from him.

"You devil!" cried Langley. "She's afraid of you. What have you been doing to her? How did she get into this state? I *will* know!"

"Gently," said Wetherall. "I can allow for your natural agitation at finding her like this, but I can't have your coming between me and *my wife*. What a faithful fellow you are, Langley. I believe you still want her—just as you did before when you thought I was dumb and blind. Come now, have

39

you got designs of *my wife*, Langley? Would you like to kiss her, caress her, take her to bed with you—my beautiful wife?"

A scarlet fury blinded Langley. He dashed an inexpert fist at the mocking face. Wetherall gripped his arm, but he broke away. Panic seized him. He fled stumbling against the furniture and rushed out. As he went he heard Wetherall very softly laughing.

The train to Paris was crowded. Langley, scrambling in at the last moment, found himself condemned to the corridor. He sat down on a suitcase and tried to think. He had not been able to collect his thoughts on his wild flight. Even now, he was not quite sure what he had fled from. He buried his head in his hands.

"Excuse me," said a polite voice.

Langley looked up. A fair man in a grey suit was looking down at him through a monocle.

"Fearfully sorry to disturb you," went on the fair man. "I'm just tryin' to barge back to my jolly old kennel. Ghastly crowd, isn't it? Don't know when I've disliked my fellow-creatures more. I say, you don't look frightfully fit. Wouldn't you be better on something more comfortable?"

Langley explained that he had not been able to get a seat. The fair man eyed his haggard and unshaven countenance for a moment and then said:

"Well, look here, why not come and lay yourself down in my bin for a bit? Have you had any grub? No? That's a mistake. Toddle along with me and we'll get hold of a spot of soup and so on. You'll excuse me mentioning it, but you look as if you'd been backing a system that's come unstuck, or something. Not my business, of course, but do have something to eat."

Langley was too faint and sick to protest. He stumbled obediently along the corridor till he was pushed into a first-class sleeper, where a rigidly correct manservant was laying out a pair of mauve silk pyjamas and a set of silver-mounted brushes.

"This gentleman's feeling rotten, Bunter," said the man with the monocle, "so I've brought him in to rest his aching head upon thy breast. Get hold of the commissariat and tell

40

'em to buzz a plate of soup along and a bottle of something drinkable."

"Very good, my lord."

Langley dropped, exhausted, on the bed, but when the food appeared he ate and drank greedily. He could not remember when he had last made a meal.

"I say," he said, "I wanted that. It's awfully decent of you. I'm sorry to appear so stupid. I've had a bit of a shock."

"Tell me all," said the stranger pleasantly.

The man did not look particularly intelligent, but he seemed friendly, and above all, normal. Langley wondered how the story would sound.

"I'm an absolute stranger to you," he began.

"And I to you," said the fair man. "The chief use of strangers is to tell things to. Don't you agree?"

"I'd like—" said Langley. "The fact is, I've run away from something. It's queer—it's—but what's the use of bothering you with it?"

The fair man sat down beside him and laid a slim hand on his arm.

"Just a moment," he said. "Don't tell me anything if you'd rather not. But my name is Wimsey—Lord Peter Wimsey— and I am interested in queer things."

It was in the middle of November when the strange man came to the village. Thin, pale and silent, with his great black hood flapping about his face, he was surrounded with an atmosphere of mystery from the start. He settled down, not at the inn, but in a dilapidated cottage high up in the mountains, and he brought with him five mule-loads of mysterious baggage and a servant. The servant was almost as uncanny as the master; he was a Spaniard and spoke Basque well enough to act as an interpreter for his employer when necessary; but his words were few, his aspect gloomy and stern, and such brief information as he vouchsafed, disquieting in the extreme. His master, he said, was a wise man; he spent all his time reading books; he ate no flesh; he was of no known country; he spoke the language of the Apostles and had talked with blessed Lazarus after his return from the grave; and when he sat alone in his chamber

41

by night, the angels of God came and conversed with him in celestial harmonies.

This was terrifying news. The few dozen villagers avoided the little cottage, especially at night-time; and when the pale stranger was seen coming down the mountain path, folded in his black robe and bearing one of his magic tomes beneath his arm, the women pushed their children within doors, and made the sign of the cross.

Nevertheless, it was a child that first made the personal acquaintance of the magician. The small son of the Widow Etcheverry, a child of bold and inquisitive disposition, went one evening adventuring into the unhallowed neighbourhood. He was missing for two hours, during which his mother, in a frenzy of anxiety, had called the neighbours about her and summoned the priest, who had unhappily been called away on business to the town. Suddenly, however, the child reappeared, well and cheerful, with a strange story to tell.

He had crept up close to the magician's house (the bold, wicked child, did ever you hear the like?) and climbed into a tree to spy upon the stranger. (Jesu-Maria!) And he saw a light in the window, and strange shapes moving about and shadows going to and fro within the room. And then there came a strain of music so ravishing it drew the very heart out of his body, as though all the stars were singing together. (Oh, my precious treasure! The wizard has stolen the heart out of him, alas! alas!) Then the cottage door opened and the wizard came out and with him a great company of familiar spirits. One of them had wings like a seraph and talked in an unknown tongue, and another was like a wee man, no higher than your knee, with a black face and a white beard, and he sat on the wizard's shoulder and whispered in his ear. And the heavenly music played louder and louder. And the wizard had a pale flame all about his head, like the pictures of the saints. (Blessed St. James of Compostella, be merciful to us all! And what then?) Why then he, the boy, had been very much frightened and wished he had not come, but the little dwarf spirit had seen him and jumped into the tree after him, climbing—oh! so fast! And he had tried to climb higher and had slipped and fallen to the ground. (Oh, the poor, wicked, brave, bad boy!)

Then the wizard had come and picked him up and spoken strange words to him and all the pain had gone away from the places where he had bumped himself (Marvellous! marvellous!), and he had carried him into the house. And inside, it was like the streets of Heaven, all gold and glittering. And the familiar spirits had sat beside the fire, nine in number, and the music had stopped playing. But the wizard's servant had brought him marvellous fruits in a silver dish, like fruits of Paradise, very sweet and delicious, and he had eaten them, and drunk a strange, rich drink from a goblet covered with red and blue jewels. Oh, yes—and there had been a tall crucifix on the wall, big, big, with a lamp burning before it and a strange sweet perfume like the smell in church on Easter Day.

(A crucifix? That was strange. Perhaps the magician was not so wicked after all. And what next?)

Next, the wizard's servant had told him not to be afraid, and had asked his name and his age and whether he could repeat his Paternoster. So he had said that prayer and the Ave Maria and part of the Credo, but the Credo was long and he had forgotten what came after *"ascendit in coelum."* So the wizard had prompted him and they had finished saying it together. And the wizard had pronounced the sacred names and words without flinching and in the right order, so far as he could tell. And then the servant had asked further about himself and his family, and he had told about the death of the black goat and about his sister's lover, who had left her because she had not so much money as the merchant's daughter. Then the wizard and his servant had spoken together and laughed, and the servant said: "My master gives this message to your sister: that where there is no love there is no wealth, but he that is bold shall have gold for the asking." And with that, the wizard had put forth his hand into the air and taken from it—out of the empty air, yes, truly—one, two, three, four, five pieces of money and given them to him. And he was afraid to take them till he had made the sign of the cross upon them, and then, as they did not vanish or turn into fiery serpents, he had taken them, and here they were!

So the gold pieces were examined and admired in fear and trembling, and then, by grandfather's advice, placed under the feet of the image of Our Lady, after a sprinkling with Holy Water for their better purification. And on the next morning, as they were still there, they were shown to the priest, who arrived, tardy and flustered upon his last night's summons, and by him pronounced to be good Spanish coin, whereof one piece being devoted to the Church to put all right with Heaven, the rest might be put to secular uses without peril to the soul. After which, the good padre made his hasty way to the cottage, and returned, after an hour, filled with good reports of the wizard.

"For, my children," said he, "this is no evil sorcerer, but a Christian man, speaking the language of the Faith. He and I have conversed together with edification. Moreover, he keeps very good wine and is altogether a very worthy person. Nor did I perceive any familiar spirits or flaming apparitions; but it is true that there is a crucifix and also a very handsome Testament with pictures in gold and colour. *Benedicite*, my children. This is a good and learned man."

And away he went back to his presbytery; and that winter the chapel of Our Lady had a new altar-cloth.

After that, each night saw a little group of people clustered at a safe distance to hear the music which poured out from the wizard's windows, and from time to time a few bold spirits would creep up close enough to peer through the chinks of the shutters and glimpse the marvels within.

The wizard had been in residence about a month, and sat one night after his evening meal in conversation with his servant. The black hood was pushed back from his head, disclosing a sleek poll of fair hair, and a pair of rather humorous grey eyes, with a cynical droop of the lids. A glass of Cockburn 1908 stood on the table at his elbow and from the arm of his chair a red-and-green parrot gazed unwinkingly at the fire.

"Time is getting on, Juan," said the magician. "This business is very good fun and all that—but is there anything doing with the old lady?"

"I think so, my lord. I have dropped a word or two here and there of marvellous cures and miracles. I think she will come. Perhaps even to-night."

"Thank goodness! I want to get the thing over before Wetherall comes back, or we may find ourselves in Queer Street. It will take some weeks, you know, before we are ready to move, even if the scheme works at all. Damn it, what's that?"

Juan rose and went into the inner room, to return in a minute carrying the lemur.

"Micky had been playing with your hair-brushes," he said indulgently. "Naughty one, be quiet! Are you ready for a little practice, my lord?"

"Oh, rather, yes! I'm getting quite a dab at this job. If all else fails, I shall try for an engagement with Maskelyn."

Juan laughed, showing his white teeth. He brought out a set of billiard-balls, coins and other conjuring apparatus, palming and multiplying them negligently as he went. The other took them from him, and the lesson proceeded.

"Hush!" said the wizard, retrieving a ball which had tiresomely slipped from his fingers in the very act of vanishing. "There's somebody coming up the path."

He pulled his robe about his face and slipped silently into the inner room. Juan grinned, removed the decanter and glasses, and extinguished the lamp. In the firelight the great eyes of the lemur gleamed strongly as it hung on the back of the high chair. Juan pulled a large folio from the shelf, lit a scented pastille in a curiously shaped copper vase and pulled forward a heavy iron cauldron which stood on the hearth. As he piled the logs about it, there came a knock. He opened the door, the lemur running at his heels.

"Whom do you seek, Mother?" he asked, in Basque.

"Is the Wise One at home?"

"His body is at home, mother; his spirit holds converse with the unseen. Enter. What would you with us?"

"I have come, as I said—ah, Mary! Is that a spirit?"

"God made spirits and bodies also. Enter and fear not."

The old woman came tremblingly forward.

"Hast though spoken with him of what I told thee?"

"I have. I have shown him the sickness of thy mistress— her husband's sufferings—all."

"What said he?"

"Nothing; he read in his book."

"Think you he can heal her?"

"I do not know; the enchantment is a strong one; but my master is mighty for good."

"Will he see me?"

"I will ask him. Remain here, and beware thou show no fear, whatever befall."

"I will be courageous," said the old woman, fingering her beads.

Juan withdrew. There was a nerve-shattering interval. The lemur had climbed up to the back of the chair again and swung, teeth-chattering, among the leaping shadows. The parrot cocked his head and spoke a few gruff words from his corner. An aromatic steam began to rise from the cauldron. Then, slowly into the red light, three, four, seven white shapes came stealthily and sat down in a circle about the hearth. Then, a faint music, that seemed to roll in from leagues away. The flame flickered and dropped. There was a tall cabinet against the wall, with gold figures on it that seemed to move with the moving firelight.

Then, out of the darkness, a strange voice chanted in an unearthly tongue that sobbed and thundered.

Martha's knees gave under her. She sank down. The seven white cats rose and stretched themselves, and came sidling slowly about her. She looked up and saw the wizard standing before her, a book in one hand and a silver wand in the other. The upper part of his face was hidden, but she saw his pale lips move and presently he spoke, in a deep, husky tone that vibrated solemnly in the dim room:

"ὦ πέπου, εἰ μὲν γὰρ, πόλεμον περὶ τόνδε
φυγόντε,
αἰεὶ δὴ μέλλοιμεν ἀγήρω τ' ἀθανάτω τε
ἔσσεθ', οὔτε κεν αὐτὸς ἐνὶ πρώτοισι μαχοίμην,
οὔτε κέ σε στέλλοιμι μάχην ἐς κυδιάνειραν..."

The great syllables went rolling on. Then the wizard paused, and added, in a kinder tone:

"Great stuff, this Homer. It goes so thunderingly as though it conjured devils. What do I do next?"

46

The servant had come back, and now whispered in Martha's ear.

"Speak now," said he. "The master is willing to help you."

Thus encouraged, Martha stammered out her request. She had come to ask the Wise Man to help her mistress, who lay under an enchantment. She had brought an offering—the best she could find, for she had not liked to take anything of her master's during his absence. But here were a silver penny, an oat-cake, and a bottle of wine, very much at the wizard's service, if such small matters could please him.

The wizard, setting aside his book, gravely accepted the silver penny, turned it magically into six gold pieces and laid the offering on the table. Over the oat-cake and the wine he showed a little hesitation, but at length, murmuring:

"Ergo omnis longo solvit se Teucria luctu"

(a line notorious for its grave spondaic cadence), he metamorphosed the one into a pair of pigeons and the other into a curious little crystal tree in a metal pot, and set them beside the coins. Martha's eyes nearly started from her head, but Juan whispered encouragingly:

"The good intention gives value to the gift. The master is pleased. Hush!"

The music ceased on a loud chord. The wizard, speaking now with greater assurance, delivered himself with fair accuracy of a page or so from Homer's Catalogue of the Ships, and, drawing from the folds of his robe his long white hand laden with antique rings, produced from mid-air a small casket of shining metal, which he proffered to the suppliant.

"The master says," prompted the servant, "that you shall take this casket, and give to your lady of the wafers which it contains, one at every meal. When all have been consumed, seek this place again. And remember to say three Aves and two Paters morning and evening for the intention of the lady's health. Thus, by faith and diligence, the cure may be accomplished."

Martha received the casket with trembling hands.

"Tendebantque manus ripae ulterioris amore," said the

wizard, with emphasis. "Poluphloisboio thalasses. Ne plus ultra. Valete. Plaudite."

He stalked away into the darkness, and the audience was over.

"It is working, then?" said the wizard to Juan.

The time was five weeks later, and five more consignments of enchanted wafers had been ceremoniously dispatched to the grim house on the mountain.

"It is working," agreed Juan. "The intelligence is returning, the body is becoming livelier and the hair is growing again."

"Thank the Lord! It was a shot in the dark, Juan, and even now I can hardly believe that anyone in the world could think of such a devilish trick. When does Wetherall return?"

"In three weeks' time."

"Then we had better fix our grand finale for to-day fortnight. See that the mules are ready, and go down to the town and get a message off to the yacht."

"Yes, my lord."

"That will give you a week to get clear with the menagerie and the baggage. And—I say, how about Martha? Is it dangerous to leave her behind, do you think?"

"I will try to persuade her to come back with us."

"Do. I should hate anything unpleasant to happen to her. The man's a criminal lunatic. Oh, lord! I'll be glad when this is over. I want to get into a proper suit of clothes again. What Bunter would say if he saw this—"

The wizard laughed, lit a cigar and turned on the gramophone.

The last act was duly staged a fortnight later.

It had taken some trouble to persuade Martha of the necessity of bringing her mistress to the wizard's house. Indeed, that supernatural personage had been obliged to make an alarming display of wrath and declaim two whole choruses from Euripides before gaining his point. The final touch was put to the terrors of the evening by a demonstration of the ghastly effects of a sodium flame—which lends a very corpse-like aspect to the human countenance, particularly in a lonely cottage on a dark night, and accompanied by incantations and the "Danse Macabre" of Saint-Saens.

Eventually the wizard was placated by a promise, and Martha departed, bearing with her a charm, engrossed upon parchment, which her mistress was to read and thereafter hang about her neck in a white silk bag.

Considered as a magical formula, the document was perhaps a little unimpressive in its language, but its meaning was such as a child could understand. It was in English, and ran:

> You have been ill and in trouble, but your friends
> are ready to cure you and help you. Don't be afraid,
> but do whatever Martha tells you, and you will soon
> be quite well and happy again.

"And even if she can't understand it," said the wizard to his man, "it can't possibly do any harm."

The events of that terrible night have become legend in the village. They tell by the fireside with bated breath how Martha brought the strange, foreign lady to the wizard's house, that she might be finally and for ever freed from the power of the Evil One. It was a dark night and a stormy one, with the wind howling terribly through the mountains.

The lady had become much better and brighter through the wizard's magic—though this, perhaps, was only a fresh glamour and delusion—and she had followed Martha like a little child on that strange and secret journey. They had crept out very quietly to elude the vigilance of old Tomaso, who had strict orders from the doctor never to let the lady stir one step from the house. As for that, Tomaso swore that he had been cast into an enchanted sleep—but who knows? There may have been no more to it than over-much wine. Martha was a cunning woman, and, some said, little better than a witch herself.

Be that as it might, Martha and the lady had come to the cottage, and there the wizard had spoken many things in a strange tongue, and the lady had spoken likewise. Yes—she who for so long had only grunted like a beast, had talked with the wizard and answered him. Then the wizard had drawn strange signs upon the floor round about the lady and himself. And when the lamp was extinguished, the signs glowed awfully, with a pale light of their own. The wizard also drew a circle about Martha herself, and warned her to keep inside it. Presently they heard a rushing noise, like great wings beating, and all the familiars leaped about, and the little white man with the black face ran up the curtain and swung from the pole. Then a voice cried out: "He comes! He comes!" and the wizard opened the door of the tall cabinet with gold images upon it, that stood in the centre of the circle, and he and the lady stepped inside it and shut the doors after them.

The rushing sound grew louder and the familiar spirits screamed and chattered—and then, all of a sudden, there was a thunder-clap and a great flash of light and the cabinet was shivered into pieces and fell down. And lo and behold! the wizard and the lady had vanished clean away and were never more seen or heard of.

This was Martha's story, told the next day to her neighbours. How she had escaped from the terrible house she could not remember. But when, some time after, a group of villagers summoned up courage to visit the place again, they found it bare and empty. Lady, wizard, servant, familiars, furniture, bags and baggage—all were gone, leaving not a trace behind them, except for a few mysterious lines and figures traced on the floor of the cottage.

This was a wonder indeed. More awful still was the disappearance of Martha herself, which took place three nights afterwards.

Next day, the American doctor returned, to find an empty hearth and a legend.

"Yacht ahoy!"

Langley peered anxiously over the rail of the *Abracadabra* as the boat loomed out of the blackness. When the first passenger came aboard, he ran hastily to greet him.

"Is it all right, Wimsey?"

"Absolutely all right. She's a bit bewildered, of course—but you needn't be afraid. She's like a child, but she's getting better every day. Bear up, old man—there's nothing to shock you about her."

Langley moved hesitatingly forward as a muffled female figure was hoisted gently on board.

"Speak to her," said Wimsey. "She may or may not recognise you. I can't say."

Langley summoned up his courage. "Good evening, Mrs. Wetherall," he said, and held out his hand.

The woman pushed the cloak from her face. Her blue eyes gazed shyly at him in the lamplight—then a smile broke out upon her lips.

"Why, I know you—of course I know you. You're Mr. Langley. I'm so glad to see you."

She clasped his hand in hers.

"Well, Langley," said Lord Peter, as he manipulated the syphon, "a more abominable crime it has never been my fortune to discover. My religious beliefs are a little ill-defined, but I hope something really beastly happens to Wetherall in the next world. Say when!

"You know, there were one or two very queer points about that story you told me. They gave me a line on the thing from the start.

"To begin with, there was this extraordinary kind of decay or imbecility settin' in on a girl in her twenties—so conveniently, too, just after you'd been hangin' round in the Wetherall home and showin' perhaps a trifle too much sensibility, don't you see? And then there was this tale of the conditions clearin' up regularly once a year or so—not like any ordinary brain-trouble. Looked as if it was being controlled by somebody.

"Then there was the fact that Mrs. Wetherall had been under her husband's medical eye from the beginning, with no family or friends who knew anything about her to keep a check on the fellow. Then there was the determined isolation of her in a place where no doctor could see her and where, even if she had a lucid interval, there wasn't a soul who could understand or be understood by her. Queer, too, that it should be a part of the world where you, with your interests, might reasonably be expected to turn up some day and be treated to a sight of what she had turned into. Then there were Wetherall's well-known researches, and the fact that he kept in touch with a chemist in London.

"All that gave me a theory, but I had to test it before I could be sure I was right. Wetherall was going to America, and that gave me a chance; but of course he left strict orders that nobody should get into or out of his house during his absence. I had, somehow, to establish an authority greater than his over old Martha, who is a faithful soul, God bless her! Hence, exit Lord Peter Wimsey and enter the magician. The treatment was tried and proved successful—hence the elopement and the rescue.

"Well, now, listen—and don't go off the deep end. It's all over now. Alice Wetherall is one of those unfortunate people who suffer from congenital thyroid deficiency. You know the thyroid gland in your throat—the one that stokes the engine and keeps the old brain going. In some people the thing doesn't work properly, and they turn out cretinous imbeciles. Their bodies don't grow and their minds don't work. But feed 'em the stuff, and they come absolutely all right—cheery and handsome and intelligent and lively as crickets. Only, don't you see, you have to *keep* feeding it to 'em, otherwise they just go back to an imbecile condition.

"Wetherall found this girl when he was a bright young student just learning about the thyroid. Twenty years ago, very few experiments had been made in this kind of treatment, but he was a bit of a pioneer. He gets hold of the kid, works a miraculous cure, and, bein' naturally bucked with himself, adopts her, gets her educated, likes the look of her, and finally marries her. You understand, don't you, that there's nothing fundamentally unsound about those thyroid deficients. Keep 'em going on the little daily dose, and they're normal in every way, fit to live an ordinary life and have ordinary healthy children.

"Nobody, naturally, knew anything about this thyroid business except the girl herself and her husband. All goes well till *you* come along. Then Wetherall gets jealous—"

"He had no cause."

Wimsey shrugged his shoulders.

"Possibly, my lad, the lady displayed a preference—we needn't go into that. Anyhow, Wetherall did get jealous and saw a perfectly marvellous revenge in his power. He carried his wife off to the Pyrenees, isolated her from all help, and then simply sat back and starved her of her thyroid extract. No doubt he told her what he was going to do, and why. It would please him to hear her desperate appeals—to let her feel herself slipping back day by day, hour by hour, into something less than a beast—"

"Oh, God!"

"As you say. Of course, after a time, a few months, she would cease to know what was happening to her. He would still have the satisfaction of watching her—seeing her skin thicken, her body coarsen, her hair fall out, her eyes grow vacant, her speech die away into mere animal noises, her brain go to mush, her habits—"

"Stop it, Wimsey."

"Well, you saw it yourself. But that wouldn't be enough for him. So, every so often, he would feed her the thyroid again and bring her back sufficiently to realise her own degradation—"

"If only I had the brute here!"

"Just as well you haven't. Well then, one day—by a stroke of luck—Mr. Langley, the amorous Mr. Langley, actually turns up. What a triumph to let him see—"

Langley stopped him again.

"Right-ho! but it was ingenious, wasn't it? So simple. The more I think of it, the more it fascinates me. But it was just that extra refinement of cruelty that defeated him. Because, when you told me the story, I couldn't help recognising the symptoms of thyroid deficiency, and I thought, 'Just supposing'—so I hunted up the chemist whose name you saw on the parcel, and, after unwinding a lot of red tape, got him to admit that he had several times sent Wetherall consignments of thyroid extract. So then I was almost sure, don't you see.

"I got a doctor's advice and a supply of gland extract, hired a tame Spanish conjurer and some performing cats and things, and barged off complete with disguise and a trick cabinet devised by the ingenious Mr. Devant. I'm a bit of a conjurer myself, and between us we didn't do so badly. The local superstitions helped, of course, and so did the gramophone records. Schubert's 'Unfinished' is first class for producing an atmosphere of gloom and mystery, so are luminous paint and the remnants of a classical education."

"Look here, Wimsey, will she get all right again?"

"Right as ninepence, and I imagine that any American court would give her a divorce on the grounds of persistent cruelty. After that—it's up to you!"

Lord Peter's friends greeted his reappearance in London with mild surprise.

"And what have *you* been doing with yourself?" demanded the Hon. Freddy Arbuthnot.

"Eloping with another man's wife," replied his lordship. "But only," he hastened to add, "in a purely Pickwickian sense. Nothing in it for yours truly. Oh, well! Let's toddle round to the Holborn Empire, and see what George Robey can do for us."

CHAPTER III
•
The Queen's Square

"You Jack o' Di'monds, you Jack o' Di'monds," said Mark Sambourne, shaking a reproachful head, "I know you of old." He rummaged beneath the white satin of his costume, panelled with gigantic oblongs and spotted to represent a set of dominoes. "Hang this fancy rig! Where the blazes has the fellow put my pockets? You rob my pocket, yes, you rob-a my pocket, you rob my pocket of silver and go-ho-hold. How much do you make it?" He extracted a fountain-pen and a chequebook.

"Five-seventeen-six," said Lord Peter Wimsey. "That's right, isn't it, partner?" His huge blue-and-scarlet sleeves rustled as he turned to Lady Hermione Creethorpe, who, in her Queen of Clubs costume, looked a very redoubtable virgin, as, indeed, she was.

"Quite right," said the old lady, "and I consider that very cheap."

"We haven't been playing long," said Wimsey apologetically.

"It would have been more, Auntie," observed Mrs. Wrayburn, "if you hadn't been greedy. You shouldn't have doubled those four spades of mine."

Lady Hermione snorted, and Wimsey hastily cut in:

"It's a pity we've got to stop, but Deverill will never forgive us if we're not there to dance Sir Roger. He feels strongly about it. What's the time? Twenty past one. Sir Roger is timed to start sharp at half-past. I suppose we'd better tootle back to the ballroom."

"I suppose we had," agreed Mrs. Wrayburn. She stood up, displaying her dress, boldly patterned with the red and black points of a backgammon board. "It's very good of you," she added, as Lady Hermione's voluminous skirts swept through the hall ahead of them, "to chuck your dancing to give Auntie her bridge. She does so hate to miss it."

"Not at all," replied Wimsey. "It's a pleasure. And in any case I was jolly glad of a rest. These costumes are dashed hot for dancing in."

"You make a splendid Jack of Diamonds, though. Such a good idea of Lady Deverill's, to make everybody come as a game. It cuts out all those wearisome pierrots and columbines." They skirted the south-west angle of the ballroom and emerged into the south corridor, lit by a great hanging lantern in four lurid colours. Under the arcading they paused and stood watching the floor, where Sir Charles Deverill's guests were foxtrotting to a lively tune discoursed by the band in the musicians' gallery at the far end. "Hullo, Giles!" added Mrs. Wrayburn, "you look hot."

"I am hot," said Giles Pomfret. "I wish to goodness I hadn't been so clever about this infernal costume. It's a beautiful billiard-table, but I can't sit down in it." He mopped his heated brow, crowned with an elegant green lamp-shade. "The only

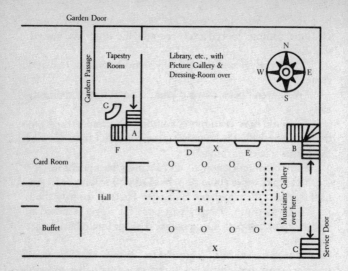

A—Stair to Dressing-Room and Gallery; B—Stair to Gallery; C—Stair to Musicians' Gallery only; D—Settee where Joan Carstairs sat; E—Settee where Jim Playfair sat; F—Where Waits stood; G—Where Ephraim Dodd sat; H—Guests' "Sir Roger"; J—Servants' "Sir Roger"; XX—Hanging Lanterns; O O O O—Arcading.

rest I can get is to hitch my behind on a radiator, and as they're all in full blast, it's not very cooling. Thank goodness, I can always make these damned sandwich boards an excuse to get out of dancing." He propped himself against the nearest column, looking martyred.

"Nina Hartford comes off best," said Mrs. Wrayburn. "Water-polo—so sensible—just a bathing-dress and a ball; though I must say it would look better on a less *Restoration* figure. Your playing-cards are much the prettiest, and I think the chess-pieces run you close. There goes Gerda Bellingham, dancing with her husband—isn't she *too* marvellous in that red wig? And the bustle and everything—my dear, so attractive. I'm glad they didn't make themselves too Lewis Carroll; Charmian Grayle is the sweetest White Queen—where is she, by the way?"

"I don't like that young woman," said Lady Hermione; "she's fast."

"Dear lady!"

"I've no doubt you think me old-fashioned. Well, I'm glad I am. I say she's fast, and, what's more, heartless. I was watching her before supper, and I'm sorry for Tony Lee. She's been flirting as hard as she can go with Harry Vibart—not to give it a worse name—and she's got Jim Playfair on a string, too. She can't even leave Frank Bellingham alone, though she's staying in his house."

"Oh, I say, Lady H!" protested Sambourne, "you're a bit hard on Miss Grayle. I mean, she's an awfully sporting kid and all that."

"I detest that word 'sporting'," snapped Lady Hermione. "Nowadays it merely means drunk and disorderly. And she's not such a kid, either, young man. In three years' time she'll be a hag, if she goes on at this rate."

"Dear Lady Hermione," said Wimsey, "we can't all be untouched by time, like you."

"You could," retorted the old lady, "if you looked after your stomachs and your morals. Here comes Frank Bellingham—looking for a drink, no doubt. Young people to-day seem to be positively pickled in gin."

The fox-trot had come to an end, and the Red King was threading his way towards them through a group of applauding couples.

"Hullo, Bellingham!" said Wimsey. "Your crown's crooked. Allow me." He set wig and head-dress to rights with skilful fingers "Not that I blame you. What crown is safe in these Bolshevik days?"

"Thanks," said Bellingham. "I say, I want a drink."

"What did I tell you?" said Lady Hermione.

"Buzz along, then, old man," said Wimsey. "You've got four minutes. Mind you turn up in time for Sir Roger."

"Right you are. Oh, I'm dancing it with Gerda, by the way. If you see her, you might tell her where I've gone to."

"We will. Lady Hermione, you're honouring me, of course?"

"Nonsense! You're not expecting me to dance at my age? The Old Maid ought to be a wallflower."

"Nothing of the sort. If only I'd had the luck to be born earlier, you and I should have appeared side by side, as Matrimony. Of course you're going to dance it with me—unless you mean to throw me over for one of these youngsters."

"I've no use for youngsters," said Lady Hermione. "No guts. Spindle-shanks." She darted a swift glance at Wimsey's scarlet hose. "You at least have some suggestion of calves. I can stand up with you without blushing for you."

Wimsey bowed his scarlet cap and curled wig in deep reverence over the gnarled knuckles extended to him.

"You make me the happiest of men. We'll show them all how to do it. Right hand, left hand, both hands across, back to back, round you go and up the middle. There's Deverill going down to tell the band to begin. Punctual old bird, isn't he? Just two minutes to go. . . . What's the matter, Miss Carstairs? Lost your partner?"

"Yes—have you seen Tony Lee anywhere?"

"The White King? Not a sign. Nor the White Queen either. I expect they're together somewhere."

"Probably. Poor old Jimmie Playfair is sitting patiently in the north corridor, looking like Casabianca."

"You'd better go along and console him," said Wimsey, laughing.

Joan Carstairs made a face and disappeared in the direction of the buffet, just as Sir Charles Deverill, giver of the party, bustled up to Wimsey and his companions, resplendent in a Chinese costume patterned with red and green dragons, bamboos, circles and characters, and carrying on his shoulder a stuffed bird with an enormous tail.

"Now, now," he exclaimed, "come along, come along, come along! All ready for Sir Roger. Got your partner, Wimsey? Ah, yes, Lady Hermione—splendid. You must come and stand next to your dear mother and me, Wimsey. Don't be late, don't be late. We want to dance it right through. The waits will begin at two o'clock—I hope they will arrive in good time. Dear me, dear me! Why aren't the servants in yet? I told Watson—I must go and speak to him."

He darted away, and Wimsey, laughing, led his partner up to the top of the room, where his mother, the Dowager Duchess of Denver, stood waiting, magnificent as the Queen of Spades.

"Ah! here you are," said the Duchess placidly. "Dear Sir Charles—he was getting quite flustered. Such a man for punctuality—he ought to have been a Royalty. A delightful party, Hermione, isn't it? Sir Roger and the waits—quite mediaeval—and a Yule-log in the hall, with the steam-radiators and everything—so oppressive!"

"Tumty, tumty, tiddledy, tumty, tumty, tiddledy," sang Lord Peter, as the band broke into the old tune. "I do adore this music. Foot it featly here and there—oh! there's Gerda Bellingham. Just a moment! Mrs. Bellingham—hi! your royal spouse awaits your Red Majesty's pleasure in the buffet. Do hurry him up. He's only got half a minute."

The Red Queen smiled at him, her pale face and black eyes startlingly brilliant beneath her scarlet wig and crown.

"I'll bring him up to scratch all right," she said, and passed on, laughing.

"So she will," said the Dowager. "You'll see that young man in the Cabinet before very long. Such a handsome couple on a public platform, and very sound, I'm told, about pigs, and that's so important, the British breakfast-table being what it is."

Sir Charles Deverill, looking a trifle heated, came hurrying back and took his place at the head of the double line of guests, which now extended three-quarters of the way down the ballroom. At the lower end, just in front of the Musicians' Gallery, the staff had filed in, to form a second Sir Roger, at right angles to the main set. The clock chimed the half-hour. Sir Charles, craning an anxious neck, counted the dancers.

"Eighteen couples. We're two couples short. How vexatious! Who are missing?"

"The Bellinghams?" said Wimsey. "No, they're here. It's the White King and Queen, Badminton and Diabolo."

"There's Badminton!" cried Mrs. Wrayburn, signalling frantically across the room. "Jim! Jim! Bother! He's gone back again. He's waiting for Charmian Grayle."

59

"Well, we can't wait any longer," said Sir Charles peevishly. "Duchess, will you lead off?"

The Dowager obediently threw her black velvet train over her arm and skipped away down the centre, displaying an uncommonly neat pair of scarlet ankles. The two lines of dancers, breaking into the hop-and-skip step of the country dance, jigged sympathetically. Below them, the cross lines of black and white and livery coats followed their example with respect. Sir Charles Deverill, dancing solemnly down after the Duchess, joined hands with Nina Hartford from the far end of the line. Tumty, tumty, tiddledy, tumty, tumty, tiddledy . . . the first couple turned outward and led the dancers down. Wimsey, catching the hand of Lady Hermione, stooped with her beneath the arch and came triumphantly up to the top of the room, in a magnificent rustle of silk and satin. "My love," sighed Wimsey, "was clad in the black velvet, and I myself in cramoisie." The old lady, well pleased, rapped him over the knuckles with her gilt sceptre. Hands clapped merrily.

"Down we go again," said Wimsey, and the Queen of Clubs and Emperor of the great Mahjongg dynasty twirled and capered in the centre. The Queen of Spades danced up to meet her Jack of Diamonds. "Bézique," said Wimsey; "double Bézique," as he gave both his hands to the Dowager. Tumty, tumty, tiddledy. He again gave his hand to the Queen of Clubs and led her down. Under their lifted arms the other seventeen couples passed. Then Lady Deverill and her partner followed them down—then five more couples.

"We're working nicely to time," said Sir Charles, with his eye on the clock. "I worked it out at two minutes per couple. Ah! here's one of the missing pairs." He waved an agitated arm. "Come into the centre—come along—in here."

A man whose head was decorated with a huge shuttlecock, and Joan Carstairs, dressed as a Diabolo, had emerged from the north corridor. Sir Charles, like a fussy rooster with two frightened hens, guided and pushed them into place between two couples who had not yet done their "hands across," and heaved a sigh of relief. It would have worried him to see them miss their turn. The clock chimed a quarter to two.

"I say, Playfair, have you seen Charmian Grayle or Tony

Lee anywhere about?" asked Giles Pomfret of the Badminton costume. "Sir Charles is quite upset because we aren't complete."

"Not a sign of 'em. I was supposed to be dancing this with Charmian, but she vanished upstairs and hasn't come down again. Then Joan came barging along looking for Tony, and we thought we'd better see it through together."

"Here are the waits coming in," broke in Joan Carstairs. "Aren't they sweet? Too-too-truly-rural!"

Between the columns on the north side of the ballroom the waits could be seen filing into place in the corridor, under the command of the Vicar. Sir Roger jigged on his exhausting way. Hands across. Down the centre and up again. Giles Pomfret, groaning, scrambled in his sandwich-boards beneath the lengthening arch of hands for the fifteenth time. Tumty, tiddledy. The nineteenth couple wove their way through the dance. Once again, Sir Charles and the Dowager Duchess, both as fresh as paint, stood at the top of the room. The clapping was loudly renewed; the orchestra fell silent; the guests broke up into groups; the servants arranged themselves in a neat line at the lower end of the room; the clock struck two; and the Vicar, receiving a signal from Sir Charles, held his tuning-fork to his ear and gave forth a sonorous A. The waits burst shrilly into the opening bars of "Good King Wenceslas."

It was just as the night was growing darker and the wind blowing stronger that a figure came thrusting its way through the ranks of the singers, and hurried across to where Sir Charles stood; Tony Lee, with his face as white as his costume.

"Charmian . . . in the tapestry room . . . dead . . . strangled."

Superintendent Johnson sat in the library, taking down the evidence of the haggard revellers, who were ushered in upon him one by one. First, Tony Lee, his haunted eyes like dark hollows in a mask of grey paper.

"Miss Grayle had promised to dance with me the last dance before Sir Roger; it was a fox-trot. I waited for her in the passage under the musicians' gallery. She never came. I did not search for her. I did not see her dancing with anyone else. When the dance was nearly over, I went out into the garden, by way of the service door under the musicians' stair. I stayed in the garden till Sir Roger de Coverley was over—"

"Was anybody with you, sir?"

"No, nobody."

"You stayed alone in the garden from—yes, from 1:20 to past 2 o'clock. Rather disagreeable, was it not, sir, with the snow on the ground?" The Superintendent glanced keenly from Tony's stained and sodden white shoes to his strained face.

"I didn't notice. The room was hot—I wanted air. I saw the waits arrive at about 1:40—I daresay they saw me. I came in a little after 2 o'clock—"

"By the service door again, sir?"

"No; by the garden door on the other side of the house, at the end of the passage which runs along beside the tapestry room. I heard singing going on in the ballroom and saw two men sitting in the little recess at the foot of the staircase on the left-hand side of the passage. I think one of them was the gardener. I went into the tapestry room—"

"With any particular purpose in mind, sir?"

"No—except that I wasn't keen on rejoining the party. I wanted to be quiet." He paused; the Superintendent said nothing. "Then I went into the tapestry room. The light was out. I switched it on and saw—Miss Grayle. She was lying close against the radiator. I thought she had fainted. I went over to her and found she was—dead. I only waited long enough to be sure, and then I went into the ballroom and gave the alarm."

"Thank you, sir. Now, may I ask, what were your relations with Miss Grayle?"

"I—I admired her very much."

"Engaged to her, sir?"

"No, not exactly."

"No quarrel—misunderstanding—anything of that sort?"

"Oh, no!"

Superintendent Johnson looked at him again, and again said nothing, but his experienced mind informed him:

"He's lying."

Aloud he only thanked and dismissed Tony. The White King stumbled drearily out, and the Red King took his place.

"Miss Grayle," said Frank Bellingham, "is a friend of my

wife and myself; she was staying at our house. Mr. Lee is also our guest. We all came in one party. I believe there was some kind of understanding between Miss Grayle and Mr. Lee—no actual engagement. She was a very bright, lively, popular girl. I have known her for about six years, and my wife has known her since our marriage. I know of no one who could have borne a grudge against Miss Grayle. I danced with her the last dance but two—it was a waltz. After that came a fox-trot and then Sir Roger. She left me at the end of the waltz; I think she said she was going upstairs to tidy. I think she went out by the door at the upper end of the ballroom. I never saw her again. The ladies' dressing-room is on the second floor, next door to the picture-gallery. You reach it by the staircase that goes up from the garden-passage. You have to pass the door of the tapestry room to get there. The only other way to the dressing-room is by the stair at the east end of the ballroom, which goes up to the picture-gallery. You would then have to pass through the picture-gallery to get to the dressing-room. I know the house well; my wife and I have often stayed here."

Next came Lady Hermione, whose evidence, delivered at great length, amounted to this:

"Chairman Grayle was a minx and no loss to anybody. I am not surprised that someone has strangled her. Women like that ought to be strangled. I would cheerfully have strangled her myself. She has been making Tony Lee's life a burden to him for the last six weeks. I saw her flirting with Mr. Vibart to-night on purpose to make Mr. Lee jealous. She made eyes at Mr. Bellingham and Mr. Playfair. She made eyes at everybody. I should think at least half a dozen people had very good reason to wish her dead."

Mr. Vibart, who arrived dressed in a gaudy Polo costume, and still ludicrously clutching a hobby-horse, said that he had danced several times that evening with Miss Grayle. She was a damn sportin' girl, rattlin' good fun. Well, a bit hot, perhaps, but, dash it all, the poor kid was dead. He might have kissed her once or twice, perhaps, but no harm in that. Well, perhaps poor old Lee did take it a bit hard. Miss Grayle liked pulling Tony's leg. He himself had liked Miss Grayle and was dashed cut-up about the whole beastly business.

Mrs. Bellingham confirmed her husband's evidence. Miss Grayle had been their guest, and they were all on the very best of terms. She felt sure that Mr. Lee and Miss Grayle had been very fond of one another. She had not seen Miss Grayle during the last three dances, but had attached no importance to that. If she had thought about it at all, she would have supposed Miss Grayle was sitting out with somebody. She herself had not been up to the dressing-room since about midnight, and had not seen Miss Grayle go upstairs. She had first missed Miss Grayle when they all stood up for Sir Roger.

Mrs. Wrayburn mentioned that she had seen Miss Carstairs in the ballroom looking for Mr. Lee, just as Sir Charles Deverill went down to speak to the band. Miss Carstairs had then mentioned that Mr. Playfair was in the north corridor, waiting for Miss Grayle. She could say for certain that the time was then 1:28. She had seen Mr. Playfair himself at 1:30. He had looked in from the corridor and gone out again. The whole party had then been standing up together, except Miss Grayle, Miss Carstairs, Mr. Lee and Mr. Playfair. She knew that, because Sir Charles had counted the couples.

Then came Jim Playfair, with a most valuable piece of evidence.

"Miss Grayle was engaged to me for Sir Roger de Coverley. I went to wait for her in the north corridor as soon as the previous dance was over. That was at 1:25. I sat on the settee in the eastern half of the corridor. I saw Sir Charles go down to speak to the band. Almost immediately afterwards, I saw Miss Grayle come out of the passage under the musicians' gallery and go up the stairs at the end of the corridor. I called out: 'Hurry up! they're just going to begin.' I do not think she heard me; she did not reply. I am quite sure I saw her. The staircase has open banisters. There is no light in that corner except from the swinging lantern in the corridor, but that is very powerful. I could not be mistaken in the costume. I waited for Miss Grayle till the dance was half over; then I gave it up and joined forces with Miss Carstairs, who had also mislaid her partner."

The maid in attendance on the dressing-room was next examined. She and the gardener were the only two servants who had not danced Sir Roger. She had not quitted the dressing-room at any time since supper, except that she might have gone as far as the door. Miss Grayle had certainly not entered the dressing-room during the last hour of the dance.

The Vicar, much worried and distressed, said that his party had arrived by the garden door at 1:40. He had noticed a man in a white costume smoking a cigarette in the garden. The waits had removed their outer clothing in the garden passage and then gone out to take up their position in the north corridor. Nobody had passed them till Mr. Lee had come in with his sad news.

Mr. Ephraim Dodd, the sexton, made an important addition to this evidence. This aged gentleman was, as he confessed, no singer, but was accustomed to go round with the waits to carry the lantern and collecting box. He had taken a seat in the garden passage "to rest me pore feet." He had seen the gentleman come in from the garden "all in white with a crown on 'is 'ead." The choir were then singing "Bring me flesh and bring me wine." The gentleman had looked about a bit, "made a face, like," and gone into the room at the foot of the stairs. He hadn't been absent "more nor a minute," when he "come out faster than he gone in," and had rushed immediately into the ballroom.

In addition to all this, there was, of course, the evidence of Dr. Pattison. He was a guest at the dance, and had hastened to view the body of Miss Grayle as soon as the alarm was given. He was of opinion that she had been brutally strangled by someone standing in front of her. She was a tall, strong girl, and he thought it would have needed a man's strength to overpower her. When he saw her at five minutes past two he concluded that she must have been killed within the last hour, but not within the last five minutes or so. The body was still quite warm, but, since it had fallen close to the hot radiator, they could not rely very much upon that indication.

Superintendent Johnson rubbed a thoughtful ear and turned to Lord Peter Wimsey, who had been able to confirm much of the previous evidence and, in particular, the exact times at which various incidents had occurred. The Superintendent knew Wimsey well, and made no bones about taking him into his confidence.

"You see how it stands, my lord. If the poor young lady was killed when Dr. Pattison says, it narrows it down a good bit. She was last seen dancing with Mr. Bellingham at—call it 1:20. At 2 o'clock she was dead. That gives us forty minutes. But if we're to believe Mr. Playfair, it narrows it down still further. He says he saw her alive just after Sir Charles went down to speak to the band, which you put at 1:28. That means that there's only five people who could possibly have done it, because all the rest were in the ballroom after that, dancing Sir Roger. There's the maid in the dressing-room; between you and me, sir, I think we can leave her out. She's a little slip of a thing, and it's not clear what motive she could have had. Besides, I've known her from a child, and she isn't the sort to do it. Then there's the gardener; I haven't seen him yet, but there again, he's a man I know well, and I'd as soon suspect myself. Well now, there's this Mr. Tony Lee, Miss Carstairs, and Mr. Playfair himself. The girl's the least probable, for physical reasons, and besides, strangling isn't a woman's crime— not as a rule. But Mr. Lee—that's a queer story, if you like. What was he doing all that time out in the garden by himself?"

"It sounds to me," said Wimsey, "as if Miss Grayle had given him the push and he had gone into the garden to eat worms."

"Exactly, my lord; and that's where his motive might come in."

"So it might," said Wimsey, "but look here. There's a couple of inches of snow on the ground. If you can confirm the time at which he went out, you ought to be able to see, from his tracks, whether he came in again before Ephraim Dodd saw him. Also, where he went in the interval and whether he was alone."

"That's a good idea, my lord. I'll send my sergeant to make inquiries."

"Then there's Mr. Bellingham. Suppose he killed her after the end of his waltz with her. Did anyone see him in the interval between that and the fox-trot?"

"Quite, my lord. I've thought of that. But you see where

that leads. It means that Mr. Playfair must have been in a conspiracy with him to do it. And from all we hear, that doesn't seem likely."

"No more it does. In fact, I happen to know that Mr. Bellingham and Mr. Playfair were not on the best of terms. You can wash that out."

"I think so, my lord. And that brings us to Mr. Playfair. It's him we're relying on for the time. We haven't found anyone who saw Miss Grayle during the dance before his—that was the fox-trot. What was to prevent him doing it then? Wait a bit. What does he say himself? Says he danced the fox-trot with the Duchess of Denver." The Superintendent's face fell, and he hunted through his notes again. "She confirms that. Says she was with him during the interval and danced the whole dance with him. Well, my lord, I suppose we can take Her Grace's word for it."

"I think you can," said Wimsey, smiling. "I've known my mother practically since my birth, and have always found her very reliable."

"Yes, my lord. Well, that brings us to the end of the fox-trot. After that, Miss Carstairs saw Mr. Playfair waiting in the north corridor. She says she noticed him several times during the interval and spoke to him. And Mrs. Wrayburn saw him there at 1:30 or thereabouts. Then at 1:45 he and Miss Carstairs came and joined the company. Now, is there anyone who can check all these points? That's the next thing we've got to see to."

Within a very few minutes, abundant confirmation was forthcoming. Mervyn Bunter, Lord Peter's personal man, said that he had been helping to take refreshments along to the buffet. Throughout the interval between the waltz and the fox-trot, Mr. Lee had been standing by the service door beneath the musicians' stair, and half-way through the fox-trot he had been seen to go out into the garden by way of the servants' hall. The police-sergeant had examined the tracks in the snow and found that Mr. Lee had not been joined by any other person, and that there was only the one set of his footprints, leaving the house by the servants' hall and returning by the garden door near the tapestry room. Several persons were also found who had seen Mr. Bellingham in the interval between the waltz and the fox-trot, and who were able to say that he had danced the fox-trot through with Mrs. Bellingham. Joan Carstairs had also been seen continuously throughout the waltz and the fox-trot, and during the following interval and the beginning of Sir. Roger. Moreover, the servants who had danced at the lower end of the room were positive that from 1:29 to 1:45 Mr. Playfair had sat continuously on the settee in the north corridor, except for the few seconds during which he had glanced into the ballroom. They were also certain that during that time no one had gone up the staircase at the lower end of the corridor, while Mr. Dodd was equally positive that, after 1:40, nobody except Mr. Lee had entered the garden passage or the tapestry room.

Finally, the circle was closed by William Hoggarty, the gardener. He asserted with the most obvious sincerity that from 1:30 to 1:40 he had been stationed in the garden passage to receive the waits and marshal them to their places. During that time, no one had come down the stair from the picture-gallery or entered the tapestry room. From 1:40 onwards, he had sat beside Mr. Dodd in the passage and nobody had passed him except Mr. Lee.

These points being settled, there was no further reason to doubt Jim Playfair's evidence, since his partners were able to prove his whereabouts during the waltz, the fox-trot and the intervening interval. At 1:28 or just after, he had seen Charmian Grayle alive. At 2:02 she had been found dead in the tapestry room. During that interval, no one had been seen to enter the room, and every person had been accounted for.

At 6 o'clock, the exhausted guests had been allowed to go to their rooms, accommodation being provided in the house for those who, like the Bellinghams, had come from a distance, since the Superintendent had announced his intention of interrogating them all afresh later in the day.

This new inquiry produced no result. Lord Peter Wimsey did not take part in it. He and Bunter (who was an expert photographer) occupied themselves in photographing the ballroom and adjacent rooms and corridors from every imaginable point of view, for, as Lord Peter said, "You never know what may turn out to be relevant." Late in the afternoon they retired together to the cellar, where with dishes, chemicals and safe-light hastily procured from the local chemist, they proceeded to develop the plates.

"That's the lot, my lord," observed Bunter at length, slosh-ing the final plate in the water and tipping it into the hypo. "You can switch the light on now, my lord."

Wimsey did so, blinking in the sudden white glare.

"A very hefty bit of work," said he. "Hullo! What's that plateful of blood you've got there?"

"That's the red backing they put on these plates, my lord, to obviate halation. You may have observed me washing it off before inserting the plate in the developing-dish. Halation, my lord, is a phenomenon—"

Wimsey was not attending.

"But why didn't I notice it before?" he demanded. "That stuff looked to me exactly like clear water."

"So it would, my lord, in the red safe-light. The appear-ance of whiteness is produced," added Bunter sententiously, "by the reflection of *all* the available light. When all the avail-able light is red, red and white are, naturally, indistinguishable. Similarly, in a green light—"

"Good God!" said Wimsey. "Wait a moment, Bunter, I must think this out. . . . Here! damn those plates—let them be. I want you upstairs."

He led the way at a canter to the ballroom, dark now, with the windows in the south corridor already curtained and only the dimness of the December evening filtering through the high windows of the clerestory above the arcading. He first turned on the great chandeliers in the ballroom itself. Owing to the heavy oak panelling that rose to the roof at both ends and all four angles of the room, these threw no light at all upon the staircase at the lower end of the north corridor. Next, he turned on the light in the four-sided hanging lantern, which hung in the north corridor above and between the two settees. A vivid shaft of green light immediately flooded the lower half of the corridor and the staircase; the upper half was bathed in strong amber, while the remaining sides of the lantern showed red towards the ballroom and blue towards the corridor wall.

Wimsey shook his head.

"Not much room for error there. Unless—I know! Run, Bunter, and ask Miss Carstairs and Mr. Playfair to come here a moment."

While Bunter was gone, Wimsey borrowed a step-ladder from the kitchen and carefully examined the fixing of the lantern. It was a temporary affair, the lantern being supported by a hook screwed into a beam and lit by means of a flex run from the socket of a permanent fixture at a little distance.

"Now, you two," said Wimsey, when the two guests arrived, "I want to make a little experiment. Will you sit down on this settee, Playfair, as you did last night. And you, Miss Carstairs—I picked you out to help because you're wearing a white dress. Will you go up the stairs at the end of the corridor as Miss Grayle did last night. I want to know whether it looks the same to Playfair as it did then—bar all the other people, of course."

He watched them as they carried out this manoeuvre. Jim Playfair looked puzzled.

"It doesn't seem quite the same, somehow. I don't know what the difference is, but there is a difference."

Joan, returning, agreed with him.

"I was sitting on that other settee part of the time," she said, "and it looks different to me. I think it's darker."

"Lighter," said Jim.

"Good!" said Wimsey. "That's what I wanted you to say. Now, Bunter, swing that lantern through a quarter-turn to the left."

The moment this was done, Joan gave a little cry.

"That's it! That's it! The blue light! I remember thinking how frosty-faced those poor waits looked as they came in."

"And you, Playfair?"

"That's right," said Jim, satisfied. "The light was red last night. *I* remember thinking how warm and cosy it looked."

Wimsey laughed.

"We're on to it, Bunter. What's the chessboard rule? *The Queen stands on a square of her own colour.* Find the maid who looked after the dressing-room, and ask her whether Mrs. Bellingham was there last night between the fox-trot and Sir Roger."

In five minutes Bunter was back with his report.

"The maid says, my lord, that Mrs. Bellingham did not come into the dressing-room at that time. But she saw her come out of the picture-gallery and run downstairs towards the tapestry room just as the band struck up Sir Roger."

"And that," said Wimsey, "was at 1:29."

"Mrs. Bellingham?" said Jim. "But you said you saw her yourself in the ballroom before 1:30. She couldn't have had time to commit the murder."

"No, she couldn't," said Wimsey. "But Charmian Grayle was dead long before that. It was the Red Queen, not the White, you saw upon the staircase. Find out why Mrs. Bellingham lied about her movements, and then we shall know the truth."

"A very sad affair, my lord," said Superintendent Johnson, some hours later. "Mr. Bellingham came across with it like a gentleman as soon as we told him we had evidence against his wife. It appears that Miss Grayle knew certain facts about him which would have been very damaging to his political career. She'd been getting money out of him for years. Earlier in the evening she surprised him by making fresh demands. During the last waltz they had together, they went into the tapestry room and a quarrel took place. He lost his temper and laid hands on her. He says he never meant to hurt her seriously, but she started to scream and he took hold of her throat to silence her and—sort of accidentally—throttled her. When he found what he'd done, he left her there and came away, feeling, as he says, all of a daze. He had the next dance with his wife. He told her what had happened, and then discovered that he'd left the little sceptre affair he was carrying in the room with the body. Mrs. Bellingham—she's a brave woman—undertook to fetch it back. She slipped through the dark passage under the musicians' gallery—which was empty—and up the stair to the picture-gallery. She did not hear Mr. Playfair speak to her. She ran through the gallery and down the other stair, secured the sceptre and hid it under her own dress. Later, she heard from Mr. Playfair about what he saw, and realised that in the red light he had mistaken her for the White Queen. In the early hours of this morning, she slipped downstairs and managed to get the lantern shifted around. Of course, she's an accessory after the fact, but she's the kind of wife a man would like to have. I hope they let her off light."

"Amen!" said Lord Peter Wimsey.

CHAPTER IV

◆

The Necklace of Pearls

Sir Septimus Shale was accustomed to assert his authority once in the year and once only. He allowed his young and fashionable wife to fill his house with diagrammatic furniture made of steel; to collect advanced artists and anti-grammatical poets; to believe in cocktails and relativity and to dress as extravagantly as she pleased; but he did insist on an old-fashioned Christmas. He was a simple-hearted man, who really liked plum-pudding and cracker mottoes, and he could not get it out of his head that other people, "at bottom," enjoyed these things also. At Christmas, therefore, he firmly retired to his country house in Essex, called in the servants to hang holly and mistletoe upon the cubist electric fittings; loaded the steel sideboard with delicacies from Fortnum & Mason; hung up stockings at the heads of the polished walnut bedsteads; and even, on this occasion only, had the electric radiators removed from the modernist grates and installed wood fires and a Yule log. He then gathered his family and friends about him, filled them with as much Dickensian good fare as he could persuade them to swallow, and, after their Christmas dinner, set them down to play "Charades" and "Clumps" and "Animal, Vegetable and Mineral" in the drawing-room, concluding these diversions by "Hide-and-Seek" in the dark all over the house. Because Sir Septimus was a very rich man, his guests fell in with this invariable programme, and if they were bored, they did not tell him so.

Another charming and traditional custom which he followed was that of presenting to his daughter Margharita a pearl on each successive birthday—this anniversary happening to coincide with Christmas Eve. The pearls now numbered twenty, and the collection was beginning to enjoy a certain celebrity, and had been photographed in the Society papers. Though not sensationally large—each one being about the size of a marrowfat pea—the pearls were of very great value. They were of exquisite colour and perfect shape and matched to a hair's weight. On this particular Christmas Eve, the presentation of the twenty-first pearl had been the occasion of a very special ceremony, There was a dance and there were speeches. On the Christmas night following, the more restricted family party took place, with the turkey and the Victorian games. There were eleven guests, in addition to Sir Septimus and Lady Shale and their daughter, nearly all related or connected to them in some way: John Shale, a brother, with his wife and their son and daughter Henry and Betty; Betty's *fiancé*, Oswald Truegood, a young man with parliamentary ambitions; George Comphrey, a cousin of Lady Shale's, aged about thirty and known as a man about town; Lavinia Prescott, asked on George's account; Joyce Trivett, asked on Henry Shale's account; Richard and Beryl Dennison, distant relations of Lady Shale, who lived a gay and expensive life in town on nobody precisely knew what resources; and Lord Peter Wimsey, asked, in a touching spirit of unreasonable hope, on Margharita's account. There were also, of course, William Norgate, secretary to Sir Septimus, and Miss Tomkins, secretary to Lady Shale, who had to be there because, without their calm efficiency, the Christmas arrangements could not have been carried through.

Dinner was over—a seemingly endless succession of soup, fish, turkey, roast beef, plum-pudding, mince-pies, crystallised fruit, nuts and five kinds of wine, presided over by Sir Septimus, all smiles, by Lady Shale, all mocking deprecation, and by Margharita, pretty and bored, with the necklace of twenty-one pearls gleaming softly on her slender throat. Gorged and dyspeptic and longing only for the horizontal position, the company had been shepherded into the drawing-room and set to play "Musical Chairs" (Miss Tomkins at the piano), "Hunt the Slipper" (slipper provided by Miss Tomkins), and "Dumb Crambo" (costumed by Miss Tomkins and Mr. William Norgate). The back drawing-room (for Sir Septimus clung to these old-fashioned names) provided an admirable dressing-room, being screened by folding doors from the large drawing-room in which the audience sat on aluminium chairs, scrabbling uneasy toes on a floor of black glass under the tremendous illumination of electricity reflected from a brass ceiling.

It was William Norgate who, after taking the temperature of the meeting, suggested to Lady Shale that they should play at something less athletic. Lady Shale agreed and, as usual, suggested bridge. Sir Septimus, as usual, blew the suggestion aside.

"Bridge? Nonsense! Nonsense! Play bridge every day of your lives. This is Christmas time. Something we can all play together. How about 'Animal, Vegetable and Mineral'?"

This intellectual pastime was a favourite with Sir Septimus; he was rather good at putting pregnant questions. After a brief discussion, it became evident that this game was an inevitable part of the programme. The party settled down to it, Sir Septimus undertaking to "go out" first and set the thing going.

Presently they had guessed among other things Miss Tomkins's mother's photograph, a gramophone record of "I want to be happy" (much scientific research into the exact composition of records, settled by William Norgate out of the *Encyclopædia Britannica*), the smallest stickleback in the stream at the bottom of the garden, the new planet Pluto, the scarf worn by Mrs. Dennison (very confusing, because it was not silk, which would be animal, or artificial silk, which would be vegetable, but made of spun glass—mineral, a very clever choice of subject), and had failed to guess the Prime Minister's wireless speech—which was voted not fair, since nobody could decide whether it was animal by nature or a kind of gas. It was decided that they should do one more word and then go on to "Hide-and Seek." Oswald Truegood had retired into the back room and shut the door behind him while the party discussed

74

the next subject of examination, when suddenly Sir Septimus broke in on the argument by calling to his daughter:

"Hullo, Margy! What have you done with your necklace?"

"I took it off, Dad, because I thought it might get broken in 'Dumb Crambo.' It's over here on this table. No, it isn't. Did you take it, Mother?"

"No, I didn't. If I'd seen it, I should have. You are a careless child."

"I believe you've got it yourself, Dad. You're teasing."

Sir Septimus denied the accusation with some energy. Everybody got up and began to hunt about. There were not many places in that bare and polished room where a necklace could be hidden. After ten minutes' fruitless investigation, Richard Dennison, who had been seated next to the table where the pearls had been placed, began to look rather uncomfortable.

"Awkward, you know," he remarked to Wimsey.

At this moment, Oswald Truegood put his head through the folding-doors and asked whether they hadn't settled on something by now, because he was getting the fidgets.

This directed the attention of the searchers to the inner room. Margharita must have been mistaken. She had taken it in there, and it had got mixed up with the dressing-up clothes somehow. The room was ransacked. Everything was lifted up and shaken. The thing began to look serious. After half an hour of desperate energy it became apparent that the pearls were nowhere to be found.

"They must be somewhere in these two rooms, you know," said Wimsey. "The back drawing-room has no door and nobody could have gone out of the front drawing-room without being seen. Unless the windows—"

No. The windows were all guarded on the outside by heavy shutters which it needed two footmen to take down and replace. The pearls had not gone out that way. In fact, the mere suggestion that they had left the drawing-room at all was disagreeable. Because—because—

It was William Norgate, efficient as ever, who coldly and boldly faced the issue.

"I think, Sir Septimus, it would be a relief to the minds of everybody present if we could all be searched."

Sir Septimus was horrified, but the guests, having found a leader, backed up Norgate. The door was locked, and the search was conducted—the ladies in the inner room and the men in the outer.

Nothing resulted from it except some very interesting information about the belongings habitually carried about by the average man and woman. It was natural that Lord Peter Wimsey should possess a pair of forceps, a pocket lens and a small folding foot-rule—was he not a Sherlock Holmes in high life? But that Oswald Truegood should have two liver-pills in a screw of paper and Henry Shale a pocket edition of *The Odes of Horace* was unexpected. Why did John Shale distend the pockets of his dress-suit with a stump of red sealing-wax, an ugly little mascot and a five-shilling piece? George Comphrey had a pair of folding scissors, and three wrapped lumps of sugar, of the sort served in restaurants and dining-cars—evidence of a not uncommon form of kleptomania; but that the tidy and exact Norgate should burden himself with a reel of white cotton, three separate lengths of string and twelve safety-pins on a card seemed really remarkable till one remembered that he had superintended all the Christmas decorations. Richard Dennison, amid some confusion and laughter, was found to cherish a lady's garter, a powder-compact and half a potato; the last-named, he said, was a prophylactic against rheumatism (to which he was subject), while the other objects belonged to his wife. On the ladies' side, the more striking exhibits were a little book on palmistry, three invisible hair-pins and a baby's photograph (Miss Tomkins); a Chinese trick cigarette-case with a secret compartment (Beryl Dennison); a *very* private letter and an outfit for mending stocking-ladders (Lavinia Prescott); and a pair of eye-brow tweezers and a small packet of white powder, said to be for headaches (Betty Shale). An agitating moment followed the production from Joyce Trivett's handbag of a small string of pearls—but it was promptly remembered that these had come out of one of the crackers at dinner-time, and they were, in fact, synthetic. In short, the search was unproductive of anything beyond a general shamefacedness and the discomfort always produced by undressing and re-dressing in a hurry at the wrong time of the day.

It was then that somebody, very grudgingly and haltingly, mentioned the horrid word "Police." Sir Septimus, naturally, was appalled by the idea. It was disgusting. He would not allow it. The pearls must be somewhere. They must search the rooms again. Could not Lord Peter Wimsey, with his experience of— er—mysterious happenings, do something to assist them?

"Eh?" said his lordship. "Oh, by Jove, yes—by all means, certainly. That is to say, provided nobody supposes—eh, what? I mean to say, you don't know that I'm not a suspicious character, do you, what?"

Lady Shale interposed with authority.

"We don't think *anybody* ought to be suspected," she said, "but, if we did, we'd know it couldn't be you. You know *far* too much about crimes to want to commit one."

"All right," said Wimsey. "But after the way the place has been gone over—" He shrugged his shoulders.

"Yes, I'm afraid you won't be able to find any footprints," said Margharita. "But we may have overlooked something."

Wimsey nodded.

"I'll try. Do you all mind sitting down on your chairs in the outer room and staying there. All except one of you—I'd better have a witness to anything I do or find. Sir Septimus— you'd be the best person, I think."

He shepherded them to their places and began a slow circuit of the two rooms, exploring every surface, gazing up to the polished brazen ceiling and crawling on hands and knees in the approved fashion across the black and shining desert of the floors. Sir Septimus followed, staring when Wimsey stared, bending with his hands upon his knees when Wimsey crawled, and puffing at intervals with astonishment and chagrin. Their progress rather resembled that of a man taking out a very inquisitive puppy for a very leisurely constitutional. Fortunately, Lady Shale's taste in furnishing made investigation easier; there were scarcely any nooks or corners where anything could be concealed.

They reached the inner drawing-room, and here the dressing-up clothes were again minutely examined, but without result. Finally, Wimsey lay down flat on his stomach to squint under a steel cabinet which was one of the few pieces of furniture which possessed short legs. Something about it seemed to catch his attention. He rolled up his sleeve and plunged his arm into the cavity, kicked convulsively in the effort to reach farther than was humanly possible, pulled out from his pocket and extended his folding foot-rule, fished with it under the cabinet and eventually succeeded in extracting what he sought.

It was a very minute object—in fact, a pin. Not an ordinary pin, but one resembling those used by entomologists to impale extremely small moths on the setting-board. It was about three-quarters of an inch in length, as fine as a very fine needle, with a sharp point and a particularly small head.

"Bless my soul!" said Sir Septimus. "What's that?"

"Does anybody here happen to collect moths or beetles or anything?" asked Wimsey, squatting on his haunches and examining the pin.

"I'm pretty sure they don't," replied Sir Septimus. "I'll ask them."

"Don't do that." Wimsey bent his head and stared at the floor, from which his own face stared meditatively back at him.

"I see," said Wimsey presently. "That's how it was done. All right, Sir Septimus. I know where the pearls are, but I don't know who took them. Perhaps it would be as well—for everybody's satisfaction—just to find out. In the meantime they are perfectly safe. Don't tell anyone that we've found this pin or that we've discovered anything. Send all these people to bed. Lock the drawing-room door and keep the key, and we'll get our man—or woman—by breakfast-time."

"God bless my soul," said Sir Septimus, very much puzzled.

Lord Peter Wimsey kept careful watch that night upon the drawing room door. Nobody, however, came near it. Either the thief suspected a trap or he felt confident that any time would do to recover the pearls. Wimsey, however, did not feel that he was wasting his time. He was making a list of people who had been left alone in the back drawing-room during the playing of "Animal, Vegetable and Mineral." The list ran as follows.

Sir Septimus Shale
Lavinia Prescott
William Norgate
Joyce Trivett and Henry Shale (together, because
    they had claimed to be incapable of guessing
    anything unaided)
Mrs. Dennison
Betty Shale
George Comphrey
Richard Dennison
Miss Tomkins
Oswald Truegood

He also made out a list of the persons to whom pearls
might be useful or desirable. Unfortunately, this list agreed in
almost all respects with the first (always excepting Sir Septimus)
and so was not very helpful. The two secretaries had both come
well recommended, but that was exactly what they would have
done had they come with ulterior designs; the Dennisons were
notorious livers from hand to mouth; Betty Shale carried mysterious white powders in her handbag, and was known to be
in with a rather rapid set in town; Henry was a harmless di-
lettante, but Joyce Trivett could twist him around her little
finger and was what Jane Austen liked to call "expensive and
dissipated"; Comphrey speculated; Oswald Truegood was rather
frequently present at Epsom and Newmarket—the search for
motives was only too fatally easy.

When the second housemaid and the under-footman appeared in the passage with household implements, Wimsey
abandoned his vigil, but he was down early to breakfast. Sir
Septimus with his wife and daughter were down before him,
and a certain air of tension made itself felt. Wimsey, standing
on the hearth before the fire, made conversation about the
weather and politics.

The party assembled gradually, but, as though by common
consent, nothing was said about pearls until after breakfast,
when Oswald Truegood took the bull by the horns.

"Well now!" said he. "How's the detective getting along?
Got your man, Wimsey?"

"Not yet," said Wimsey easily.

Sir Septimus, looking at Wimsey as though for his cue, cleared his throat and dashed into speech.

"All very tiresome," he said, "all very unpleasant. Hr'rm. Nothing for it but the police, I'm afraid. Just at Christmas, too. Hr'rm. Spoilt the party. Can't stand seeing all this stuff about the place." He waved his hands towards the festoons of evergreens and coloured paper that adorned the walls. "Take it all down, eh, what? No heart in it. Hr'rm. Burn the lot."

"What a pity, when we worked so hard over it," said Joyce.

"Oh, leave it, Uncle," said Henry Shale. "You're bothering too much about the pearls. They're sure to turn up."

"Shall I ring for James?" suggested William Norgate.

"No," interrupted Comphrey, "let's do it ourselves. It'll give us something to do and take our minds off our troubles."

"That's right," said Sir Septimus. "Start right away. Hate the sight of it."

He savagely hauled a great branch of holly down from the mantel-piece and flung it, crackling, into the fire.

"That's the stuff," said Richard Dennison. "Make a good old blaze!" He leapt up from the table and snatched the mistletoe from the chandelier. "Here goes! One more kiss for somebody before it's too late."

"Isn't it unlucky to take it down before the New Year?" suggested Miss Tomkins.

"Unlucky be hanged. We'll have it all down. Off the stairs and out of the drawing-room too. Somebody go and collect it."

"Isn't the drawing-room locked?" asked Oswald.

"No. Lord Peter says the pearls aren't there, wherever else they are, so it's unlocked. That's right, isn't it, Wimsey?"

"Quite right. The pearls were taken out of these rooms. I can't tell yet how, but I'm positive of it. In fact, I'll pledge my reputation that wherever they are, they're not up there."

"Oh, well," said Comphrey, "in that case, have at it! Come along, Lavinia—you and Dennison do the drawing-room and I'll do the back room. We'll have a race."

"But if the police are coming in," said Dennison, "oughtn't everything to be left just as it is?"

"Damn the police!" shouted Sir Septimus. "They don't want evergreens."

Oswald and Margharita were already pulling the holly and ivy from the staircase, amid peals of laughter. The party dispersed. Wimsey went quietly upstairs and into the drawing-room, where the work of demolition was taking place at a great rate, George having bet the other two ten shillings to a tanner that they would not finish their part of the job before he finished his.

"You mustn't help," said Lavinia, laughing to Wimsey. "It wouldn't be fair."

Wimsey said nothing, but waited till the room was clear. Then he followed them down again to the hall, where the fire was sending up a great roaring and spluttering, suggestive of Guy Fawkes night. He whispered to Sir Septimus, who went forward and touched George Comphrey on the shoulder.

"Lord Peter wants to say something to you, my boy," he said.

Comphrey started and went with him a little reluctantly, as it seemed. He was not looking very well.

"Mr. Comphrey," said Wimsey, "I fancy these are some of your property." He held out the palm of his hand, in which rested twenty-two fine, small-headed pins.

"Ingenious," said Wimsey, "but something less ingenious would have served his turn better. It was very unlucky, Sir Septimus, that you should have mentioned the pearls when you did. Of course, he hoped that the loss wouldn't be discovered till we'd chucked guessing games and taken to 'Hide-and-Seek.' Then the pearls might have been anywhere in the house, we shouldn't have locked the drawing-room door, and he could have recovered them at his leisure. He had had this possibility in his mind when he came here, obviously, and that was why he brought the pins, and Miss Shale's taking off the necklace to play 'Dumb Crambo' gave him his opportunity.

"He had spent Christmas here before, and knew perfectly well that 'Animal, Vegetable and Mineral' would form part of the entertainment. He had only to gather up the necklace from the table when it came to his turn to retire, and he knew he

81

could count on at least five minutes by himself while we were all arguing about the choice of a word. He had only to snip the pearls from the string with his pocket-scissors, burn the string in the grate and fasten the pearls to the mistletoe with the fine pins. The mistletoe was hung on the chandelier, pretty high—it's a lofty room—but he could easily reach it by standing on the glass table, which wouldn't show footmarks, and it was almost certain that nobody would think of examining the mistletoe for extra berries. I shouldn't have thought of it myself if I hadn't found that pin which he had dropped. That gave me the idea that the pearls had been separated and the rest was easy. I took the pearls off the mistletoe last night—the clasp was there, too, pinned among the holly-leaves. Here they are. Comphrey must have got a nasty shock this morning. I knew he was our man when he suggested that the guests should tackle the decorations themselves and that he should do the back drawing-room—but I wish I had seen his face when he came to the mistletoe and found the pearls gone."

"And you worked it all out when you found the pin?" said Sir Septimus.

"Yes; I knew then where the pearls had gone to."

"But you never even looked at the mistletoe."

"I saw it reflected in the black glass floor, and it struck me then how much the mistletoe berries looked like pearls."

Part Two

MONTAGUE EGG STORIES
•

CHAPTER I

◆

The Poisoned Dow '08

"Good morning, miss," said Mr. Montague Egg, removing his smart trilby with something of a flourish as the front door opened. "Here I am again, you see. Not forgotten me, have you? That's right, because I couldn't forget a young lady like you, not in a hundred years. How's his lordship to-day? Think he'd be willing to see me for a minute or two?"

He smiled pleasantly, bearing in mind Maxim Number Ten of the *Salesman's Handbook*, "The goodwill of the maid is nine-tenths of the trade."

The parlourmaid, however, seemed nervous and embarrassed.

"I don't—oh, yes—come in, please. His lordship—that is to say—I'm afraid—"

Mr. Egg stepped in promptly, sample case in hand, and, to his great surprise, found himself confronted by a policeman, who, in somewhat gruff tones, demanded his name and business.

"Travelling representative of Plummet & Rose, Wines and Spirits, Piccadilly," said Mr. Egg, with the air of one who has nothing to conceal. "Here's my card. What's up, sergeant?"

"Plummet & Rose?" said the policeman. "Ah, well, just sit down a moment, will you? The inspector'll want to have a word with you, I shouldn't wonder."

More and more astonished, Mr Egg obediently took a seat, and in a few minutes' time found himself ushered into a small sitting-room which was occupied by a uniformed police inspector and another policeman with a note-book.

"Ah!" said the inspector. "Take a seat, will you, Mr.—ha, hum—Egg. Perhaps you can give us a little light on this affair.

Do you know anything about a case of port wine that was sold to Lord Borrodale last spring?"

"Certainly I do," replied Mr. Egg. "if you mean the Dow '08. I made the sale myself. Six dozen at 192s. a dozen. Ordered from me, personally, March 3rd. Dispatched from our head office March 8th. Receipt acknowledged March 10th, with cheque in settlement. All in order our end. Nothing wrong with it, I hope? We've had no complaint. In fact, I've just called to ask his lordship how he liked it and to ask if he'd care to place a further order."

"I see," said the inspector. "You just happened to call today in the course of your usual round? No special reason?"

Mr. Egg, now convinced that something was very wrong indeed, replied by placing his order-book and road schedule at the inspector's disposal.

"Yes," said the inspector, when he had glanced through them. "That seems to be all right. Well, now, Mr. Egg, I'm sorry to say that Lord Borrodale was found dead in his study this morning under circumstances strongly suggestive of his having taken poison. And what's more, it looks very much as if the poison had been administered to him in a glass of this port wine of yours."

"You don't say!" said Mr. Egg incredulously. "I'm very sorry to hear that. It won't do us any good, either. Not but what the wine was wholesome enough when we sent it out. Naturally, it wouldn't pay us to go putting anything funny into our wines; I needn't tell you that. But it's not the sort of publicity we care for. What makes you think it was the port, anyway?"

For answer, the inspector pushed over to him a glass decanter which stood upon the table.

"See what you think yourself. It's all right—we've tested it for fingerprints already. Here's a glass if you want one, but I shouldn't advise you to swallow anything—not unless you're fed up with life."

Mr. Egg took a cautious sniff at the decanter and frowned. He poured out a thimbleful of the wine, sniffed and frowned again. Then he took an experimental drop upon his tongue, and immediately expectorated, with the utmost possible delicacy, into a convenient flower-pot.

"Oh, dear, oh, dear," said Mr. Montague Egg. His rosy face was puckered with distress. "Tastes to me as though the old gentleman had been dropping his cigar-ends into it."

The inspector exchanged a glance with the policeman.

"You're not far out," he said. "The doctor hasn't quite finished his post-mortem, but he says it looks to him like nicotine poisoning. Now, here's the problem. Lord Borrodale was accustomed to drink a couple of glasses of port in his study every night after dinner. Last night the wine was taken in to him as usual at 9 o'clock. It was a new bottle, and Craven— that's the butler—brought it straight up from the cellar in a basket arrangement—"

"A cradle," interjected Mr. Egg.

"—a cradle, if that's what you call it. James the footman followed him, carrying the decanter and a wineglass on a tray. Lord Borrodale inspected the bottle, which still bore the original seal, and then Craven drew the cork and decanted the wine in full view of Lord Borrodale and the footman. Then both servants left the room and retired to the kitchen quarters, and as they went, they heard Lord Borrodale lock the study door after them."

"What did he do that for?"

"It seems he usually did. He was writing his memoirs— he was a famous judge, you know—and as some of the papers he was using were highly confidential, he preferred to make himself safe against sudden intruders. At 11 o'clock, when the household went to bed, James noticed that the light was still on in the study. In the morning, it was discovered that Lord Borrodale had not been to bed. The study door was still locked and, when it was broken open, they found him lying dead on the floor. It looked as though he had been taken ill, had tried to reach the bell, and had collapsed on the way. The doctor says he must have died at about 10 o'clock."

"Suicide?" suggested Mr. Egg.

"Well, there are difficulties about that. The position of the body, for one thing. Also, we've carefully searched the room and found no traces of any bottle or anything that he could have kept the poison in. Besides, he seems to have enjoyed his life. He had no financial or domestic worries, and in spite of his advanced age his health was excellent. Why should he commit suicide?"

"But if he didn't," objected Mr. Egg, "how was it he didn't notice the bad taste and smell of the wine?"

"Well, he seems to have been smoking a pretty powerful cigar at the time," said the inspector (Mr. Egg shook a reproachful head), "and I'm told he was suffering from a slight cold, so that his taste and smell may not have been in full working order. There are no fingerprints on the decanter or the glass except his own and those of the butler and the footman—though, of course, that wouldn't prevent anybody dropping poison into either of them, if only the door hadn't been locked. The windows were both fastened on the inside, too, with burglar-proof catches."

"How about the decanter?" asked Mr. Egg, jealous for the reputation of his firm. "Was it clean when it came in?"

"Yes, it was. James washed it out immediately before it went into the study; the cook swears she saw him do it. He used water from the tap and then swilled it round with a drop of brandy."

"Quite right," said Mr. Egg approvingly.

"And there's nothing wrong with the brandy, either, for Craven took a glass of it himself afterwards—to settle his palpitations, so he says." The inspector sniffed meaningly. "The glass was wiped out by James when he put it on the tray, and then the whole thing was carried along to the study. Nothing was put down or left for a moment between leaving the pantry and entering the study, but Craven recollects that as he was crossing the hall Miss Waynfleet stopped him and spoke to him for a moment about some arrangements for the following day."

"Miss Waynfleet? That's the niece, isn't it? I saw her on my last visit. A very charming young lady."

"Lord Borrodale's heiress," remarked the inspector meaningly.

"A very *nice* young lady," said Mr. Egg, with emphasis. "And I understand you to say that Craven was carrying only the candle, not the decanter or the glass."

"That's so."

"Well, then, I don't see that she could have put anything

into what James was carrying." Mr. Egg paused. "The seal on the cork, now—you say Lord Borrodale saw it?"

"Yes, and so did Craven and James. You can see it for yourself, if you like—what's left of it."

The inspector produced an ash-tray, which held a few fragments of dark blue sealing-wax, together with a small quantity of cigar-ash. Mr. Egg inspected them carefully.

"That's our wax and our seal, all right," he pronounced. "The top of the cork has been sliced off cleanly with a sharp knife and the mark's intact. 'Plummet & Rose. Dow 1908.' Nothing wrong with that. How about the strainer?"

"Washed out that same afternoon in boiling water by the kitchenmaid. Wiped immediately before using by James, who brought it in on the tray with the decanter and the glass. Taken out with the bottle and washed again at once, unfortunately— otherwise, of course, it might have told us something about when the nicotine got into the port wine."

"Well," said Mr. Egg obstinately, "it didn't get in at our place, that's a certainty. What's more, I don't believe it ever was in the bottle at all. How could it be? Where is the bottle, by the way?"

"It's just been packed up to go to the analyst, I think," said the inspector, "but as you're here, you'd better have a look at it. Podgers, let's have that bottle again. There are no fingerprints on it except Craven's, by the way, so it doesn't look as if it had been tampered with."

The policeman produced a brown paper parcel, from which he extracted a port-bottle, its mouth plugged with a clean cork. Some of the original dust of the cellar still clung to it, mingled with fingerprint powder. Mr. Egg removed the cork and took a long, strong sniff at the contents. Then his face changed.

"Where did you get this bottle from?" he demanded sharply.

"From Craven. Naturally, it was one of the first things we asked to see. He took us along to the cellar and pointed it out."

"Was it standing by itself or with a lot of other bottles?"

"It was standing on the cellar floor at the end of a row of empties, all belonging to the same bin; he explained that he put them on the floor in the order in which they were used, till the time came for them to be collected and taken away."

Mr. Egg thoughtfully tilted the bottle; a few drops of thick red liquid, turbid with disturbed crust, escaped into his wine-glass. He smelt them again and tasted them. His snub nose looked pugnacious.

"Well?" asked the inspector.

"No nicotine there, at all events," said Mr. Egg, "unless my nose deceives me, which, you will understand, inspector, isn't likely, my nose being my livelihood, so to speak. No. You'll have to send it to be analysed of course; I quite understand that, but I'd be ready to bet quite a little bit of money you'll find that bottle innocent. And that, I needn't tell you, will be a great relief to our minds. And I'm sure, speaking for myself, I very much appreciate the kind way you've put the matter before me."

"That's all right; your expert knowledge is of value. We can probably now exclude the bottle straight away and concentrate on the decanter."

"Just so," replied Mr. Egg. "Ye-es. Do you happen to know how many of the six dozen bottles had been used?"

"No, but Craven can tell us, if you really want to know."

"Just for my own satisfaction," said Mr. Egg. "Just to be sure that this *is* the right bottle, you know. I shouldn't like to feel I might have misled you in any way."

The inspector rang the bell, and the butler promptly appeared—an elderly man of intensely respectable appearance.

"Craven," said the inspector, "this is Mr. Egg of Plummet & Rose's."

"I am already acquainted with Mr. Egg."

"Quite. He is naturally interested in the history of the port wine. He would like to know—what is it, exactly, Mr. Egg?"

"This bottle, said Monty, rapping it lightly with his finger-nail, "it's the one you opened last night?"

"Yes, sir."

"Sure of that?"

"Yes, sir."

"How many dozen have you got left?"

"I couldn't say off-hand, sir, without the cellarbook."

"And that's in the cellar, eh? I'd like to have a look at your cellars—I'm told they're very fine. All in apple-pie order, I'm sure. Right temperature and all that?"

"Undoubtedly, sir."

"We'll all go and look at the cellar," suggested the inspector, who in spite of his expressed confidence seemed to have doubts about leaving Mr. Egg alone with the butler.

Craven bowed and led the way, pausing only to fetch the keys from his pantry.

"This nicotine, now," prattled Mr. Egg, as they proceeded down a long corridor, "is it very deadly? I mean, would you require a great quantity of it to poison a person?"

"I understand from the doctor," replied the inspector, "that a few drops of the pure extract, or whatever they call it, would produce death in anything from twenty minutes to seven or eight hours."

"Dear, dear!" said Mr. Egg. "And how much of the port had the poor old gentleman taken? The full two glasses?"

"Yes, sir; to judge by the decanter, he had. Lord Borrodale had the habit of drinking his port straight off. He did not sip it, sir."

Mr. Egg was distressed.

"Not the right thing at all," he said mournfully. "No, no. Smell, sip and savour to bring out the flavour—that's the rule for wine, you know. Is there such a thing as a pond or stream in the garden, Mr. Craven?"

"No, sir," said the butler, a little surprised.

"Ah! I was just wondering. Somebody must have brought the nicotine along in something or other, you know. What would they do afterwards with the little bottle or whatever it was?"

"Easy enough to throw it in among the bushes or bury it, surely," said Craven. "There's six acres of garden, not counting the meadow or the courtyard. Or there are the water-butts, of course, or the well."

"How stupid of me," confessed Mr. Egg. "I never thought of that. Ah! this is the cellar, is it? Splendid—a real slap-up outfit, I call this. Nice, even temperature, too. Same summer and winter, eh? Well away from the house-furnace?"

"Oh, yes, indeed, sir. That's the other side of the house.

Be careful of the last step, gentlemen; it's a little broken away. Here is where the Dow '08 stood, sir. No. 17 bin—one, two, three and a half dozen remaining, sir."

Mr. Egg nodded and, holding his electric torch close to the protruding necks of the bottles, made a careful examination of the seals.

"Yes," he said, "here they are. Three and a half dozen, as you say. Sad to think that the throat they should have gone down lies, as you might say, closed up by Death. I often think, as I make my rounds, what a pity it is we don't all grow mellower and softer in our old age, same as this wine. A fine old gentleman, Lord Borrodale, or so I'm told, but something of a tough nut, if that's not disrespectful."

"He was hard, sir," agreed the butler, "but just. A very just master."

"Quite," said Mr. Egg. "And these, I take it, are the empties. Twelve, twenty-four, twenty-nine—and one is thirty—and three and a half dozen is forty-two—seventy-two—six dozen—that's O.K. by me." He lifted the empty bottles one by one. "They say dead men tell no tales, but they talk to little Monty Egg all right. This one, for instance. If this ever held Plummet & Rose's Dow '08 you can take Monty Egg and scramble him. Wrong smell, wrong crust, and that splash of whitewash was never put on by our cellar-man. Very easy to mix up one empty bottle with another. Twelve, twenty-four, twenty-eight and one is twenty-nine. I wonder what's become of the thirtieth bottle."

"I'm sure I never took one away," said the butler.

"The pantry keys—on a nail inside the door—very accessible," said Monty.

"Just a moment," interrupted the inspector. "Do you say that that bottle doesn't belong to the same bunch of port wine?"

"No, it doesn't—but no doubt Lord Borrodale sometimes went in for a change of vintage." Mr. Egg inverted the bottle and shook it sharply. "Quite dry. Curious. Had a dead spider at the bottom of it. You'd be surprised how long a spider can exist without food. Curious that this empty bottle, which comes in the middle of the row, should be drier than the one at the beginning of the row, and should contain a dead spider. We see a deal of curious things in our calling, inspector—we're encouraged to notice things, as you might say. 'The salesman with the open eye sees commissions mount up high.' You might call this bottle a curious thing. And here's another. That other bottle, the one you said was opened last night, Craven—how did you come to make a mistake like that? If my nose is to be trusted, not to mention my palate, that bottle's been open a week at least."

"Has it indeed, sir? I'm sure it's the one as I put here at the end of this row. Somebody must have been and changed it."

"But—" said the inspector. He stopped in mid-speech, as though struck by a sudden thought. "I think you'd better let me have those cellar keys of yours, Craven, and we'll get this cellar properly examined. That'll do for the moment. If you'll just step upstairs with me, Mr. Egg, I'd like a word with you."

"Always happy to oblige," said Monty agreeably. They returned to the upper air.

"I don't know if you realise, Mr. Egg," observed the inspector, "the bearing, or, as I might say, the inference of what you said just now. Supposing you're right about this bottle not being the right one, somebody's changed it on purpose, and the right one's missing. And, what's more, the person that changed the bottle left no fingerprints behind him—or her."

"I see what you mean," said Mr. Egg, who had indeed drawn this inference some time ago, "and what's more, it looks as if the poison had been in the bottle after all, doesn't it? And that—you're going to say—is a serious look-out for Plummet & Rose, seeing there's no doubt our seal was on the bottle when it was brought into Lord Borrodale's room. I don't deny it, inspector. It's useless to bluster and say 'No, no,' when it's perfectly clear that the facts are so. That's a very useful motto for a man that wants to get on in our line of business."

"Well, Mr. Egg," said the inspector, laughing, "what will you say to the next inference? Since nobody but you had any interest in changing that bottle over, it looks as though I ought to clap the handcuffs on you."

"Now, that's a disagreeable sort of an inference," protested Mr. Egg, "and I hope you won't follow it up. I shouldn't like anything of that sort to happen, and my employers wouldn't fancy it either. Don't you think that, before we do anything we might have cause to regret, it would be a good idea to have a look in the furnace-room?"

"Why the furnace-room?"

"Because," said Mr. Egg, "it's the place that Craven particularly didn't mention when we were asking him where anybody might have put a thing he wanted to get rid of."

The inspector appeared to be struck by this line of reasoning. He enlisted the aid of a couple of constables, and very soon the ashes of the furnace that supplied the central heating were being assiduously raked over. The first find was a thick mass of semi-molten glass, which looked as though it might once have been part of a wine bottle.

"Looks as though you might be right," said the inspector, "but I don't see how we're to prove anything. We're not likely to get any nicotine out of this."

"I suppose not," agreed Mr. Egg sadly. "But"—his face brightened—"how about this?"

From the sieve in which the constable was sifting the ashes he picked out a thin piece of warped and twisted metal, to which a lump of charred bone still clung.

"What on earth's that?"

"It doesn't look like much, but I think it might once have been a corkscrew," suggested Mr. Egg mildly. "There's something homely and familiar about it. And, if you'll look here, I think you'll see that the metal part of it is hollow. And I shouldn't be surprised if the thick bone handle was hollow, too. It's very badly charred, of course, but if you were to split it open, and if you were to find a hollow inside it, and possibly a little melted rubber—well, that might explain a lot."

The inspector smacked his thigh.

"By Jove, Mr. Egg!" he exclaimed, "I believe I see what you're getting at. You mean that if this corkscrew had been made hollow, and contained a rubber reservoir, inside, like a fountain-pen, filled with poison, the poison might be made to flow down the hollow shaft by pressure on some sort of plunger arrangement."

"That's it," said Mr. Egg. "It would have to be screwed

into the cork very carefully, of course, so as not to damage the tube, and it would have to be made long enough to project beyond the bottom of the cork, but still, it might be done. What's more, it has been done, or why should there be this little hole in the metal, about a quarter of an inch from the tip? Ordinary corkscrews never have holes in them—not in my experience, and I've been, as you might say, brought up on corkscrews."

"But who, in that case—?"

"Well, the man who drew the cork, don't you think? The man whose fingerprints were on the bottle."

"Craven? But where's his motive?"

"I don't know," said Mr. Egg, "but Lord Borrodale was a judge, and a hard judge too. If you were to have Craven's fingerprints sent up to Scotland Yard, they might recognise them. I don't know. It's possible, isn't it? Or maybe Miss Waynfleet might know something about him. Or he might just possibly be mentioned in Lord Borrodale's memoirs that he was writing."

The inspector lost no time in following up this suggestion. Neither Scotland Yard nor Miss Waynfleet had anything to say against the butler, who had been two years in his situation and had always been quite satisfactory, but a reference to the records of Lord Borrodale's judicial career showed that, a good many years before, he had inflicted a savage sentence of penal servitude on a young man called Craven, who was by trade a skilled metal-worker and had apparently been involved in a fraud upon his employer. A little further investigation showed that this young man had been released from prison six months previously.

"Craven's son, of course," said the inspector. "And he had the manual skill to make the corkscrew in exact imitation of the one ordinarily used in the household. Wonder where they got the nicotine from? Well, we shall soon be able to check that up. I believe it's not difficult to obtain it for use in the garden. I'm very much obliged to you for your expert assistance, Mr. Egg. It would have taken us a long time to get to the rights and wrongs of those bottles. I suppose, when you found that

Craven had given you the wrong one, you began to suspect him?"

"Oh, no," said Mr. Egg, with modest pride, "I knew it was Craven the minute he came into the room."

"No, did you? You're a regular Sherlock, aren't you? But why?"

"He called me 'sir,'" explained Mr. Egg, coughing delicately. "Last time I called he addressed me as 'young fellow' and told me that tradesmen must go round to the back door. A bad error of policy. 'Whether you're wrong or whether your right, it's always better to be polite,' as it says in the *Salesman's Handbook*."

CHAPTER II
◆
Sleuths on the Scent

The commercial room at the Pig and Pewter presented to Mr. Montague Egg the aspect of a dim cavern in which some primaeval inhabitant had been cooking his mammoth-meat over a fire of damp seaweed. In other words, it was ill lit, cold, smoky and permeated with an odour of stale food.

"Oh dear, oh dear!" muttered Mr. Egg. He poked at the sullen coals, releasing a volume of pea-coloured smoke which made him cough.

Mr. Egg rang the bell.

"Oh, if you please, sir," said the maid who answered the summons, "I'm sure I'm very sorry, but it's always this way when the wind's in the east, sir, and we've tried ever so many sorts of cowls and chimney-pots, you'd be surprised. The man was here to-day a-working in it, which is why the fire wasn't lit till just now, sir, but they don't seem able to do nothink with it. But there's a beautiful fire in the bar-parlour, sir, if you cared to step along. There's a very pleasant party in there, sir. I'm sure you would be comfortable. There's another commercial gentleman like yourself, sir, and old Mr. Faggott and Sergeant Jukes over from Drabblesford. Oh, and there's two parties of motorists, but they're all quite nice and quiet, sir."

"That'll suit me all right," said Mr. Egg amiably. But he made a mental note, nevertheless, that he would warn his fellow-commercials against the Pig and Pewter at Mugbury, for an inn is judged by its commercial room. Moreover, the dinner had been bad, with a badness not to be explained by his own rather late arrival.

In the bar-parlour, however, things were better. At one side of the cheerful hearth sat old Mr. Faggott, an aged countryman, beneath whose scanty white beard dangled a long, scarlet comforter. In his hand was a tankard of ale. Opposite to him, also with a tankard, was a large man, obviously a policeman in mufti. At a table in front of the fireplace sat an alert-looking, darkish, youngish man whom Mr. Egg instantly identified as the commercial gentleman by the stout leather bag at his side. He was drinking sherry. A young man and a girl in motor-cycling kit were whispering together at another table, over a whisky-and-polly and a glass of port. Another man, with his hat and burberry on, was ordering Guinness at the little serving-hatch which communicated with the bar, while, in a far corner, an indeterminate male figure sat silent and half concealed by a slouch hat and a newspaper. Mr. Egg saluted the company with respect and observed that it was a nasty night.

The commercial gentleman uttered an emphatic agreement.

"I ought to have got on to Drabblesford to-night," he added, "but with this frost and drizzle and frost again the roads are in such a state, I think I'd better stay where I am."

"Same here," said Mr. Egg, approaching the hatch. "Half of mild-and-bitter, please. Cold, too, isn't it?"

"Very cold," said the policeman.

"Ar," said old Mr. Faggott.

"Foul," said the man in the burberry, returning from the hatch and seating himself near the commercial gentleman. "I've reason to know it. Skidded into a telegraph-pole two miles out. You should see my bumpers. Well! I suppose it's only to be expected this time of year."

97

"Ar!" said old Mr. Faggott. There was a pause.

"Well," said Mr. Egg, politely raising his tankard, "here's luck!"

The company acknowledged the courtesy in a suitable manner, and another pause followed. It was broken by the traveller.

"Acquainted with this part of the country, sir?"

"Why, no," said Monty Egg. "It's not my usual beat. Bastable covers it as a rule—Henry Bastable—perhaps you know him? He and I travel for Plummet & Rose, wines and spirits."

"Tall, red-haired fellow?"

"That's him. Laid up with rheumatic fever, poor chap, so I'm taking over temporarily. My name's Egg—Montague Egg."

"Oh, yes, I think I've heard of you from Taylor of Harrogate Bros. Redwood is my name. Fragonard & Co., perfumes and toilet accessories."

Mr. Egg bowed and inquired, in a discreet and general way, how Mr. Redwood was finding things.

"Not too bad. Of course, money's a bit tight; that's only to be expected. But, considering everything, not too bad. I've got a line here, by the way, which is doing pretty well and may give *you* something to think about." He bent over, unstrapped his bag and produced a tall flask, its glass stopper neatly secured with a twist of fine string. "Tell me what you think of that." He removed the string and handed the sample to Monty.

"Parma violet?" said that gentleman, with a glance at the label. "The young lady should be the best judge of this. Allow me, miss. Sweets to the sweet," he added gallantly. "You'll excuse me, I'm sure."

The girl giggled.

"Go on, Gert," said her companion. "Never refuse a good offer." He removed the stopper and sniffed heartily at the perfume. "This is high-class stuff, this is. Put a drop on your handkerchief. Here—I'll do it for you!"

"Oh! it's lovely!" said the girl. "Refined, I call it. Get along, Arthur, do! Leave my handkerchief alone—what they'll all think of you! I'm sure this gentleman won't mind you having a drop for yourself if you want it."

Arthur favoured the company with a large wink, and sprinkled his handkerchief liberally. Monty rescued the flask and passed it to the man in the burberry.

"Excuse me, sir," said Mr. Redwood, "but if I might point it out, it's not everybody knows the right way to test perfume. Just dab a little on the hand, wait while the liquid evaporates, and then raise the hand to the nostrils."

"Like this?" said the man in the burberry, dexterously hitching the stopper out with his little finger, pouring a drop of perfume into his left palm and re-stoppering the bottle, all in one movement. "Yes, I see what you mean."

"That's very interesting," said Monty, much impressed and following the example set him. "Same as when you put old brandy in a thin glass and cradle it in the hollow of the palm to bring out the aroma. The warmth of the hand makes the ethers expand. I'm very glad to know from you, Mr. Redmond, what is the correct method with perfumes. Ready to learn means ready to earn—that's Monty Egg, every time. A very fine perfume indeed. Would you like to try it, sir?"

He offered the bottle first to the aged countryman (who shook his head, remarking acidly that he "couldn't abide smells and sick nastiness") and then to the policeman, who, disdaining refinements, took a strong sniff at the bottle and pronounced the scent "good, but a bit powerful for his liking."

"Well, well, tastes differ," said Monty. He glanced round, and, observing the silent man in the far corner, approached him confidently with a request for his opinion.

"What the devil's the matter with *you?*" growled this person, emerging reluctantly from behind his barricade of newspaper, and displaying a bristling and bellicose fair moustache and a pair of sulky blue eyes. "There seems to be no peace in this bar. Scent? Can't abide the stuff." He snatched the perfume impatiently from Mr. Egg's hand, sniffed and thrust the stopper back with such blind and fumbling haste that it missed the neck of the flask altogether and rolled away under the table. "Well, it's scent. What else do you want me to say about it? I'm not going to buy it, if that's what you're after."

"Certainly not, sir," said Mr. Redwood, hurt, and hastening to retrieve his scattered property. "Wonder what's bitten him," he continued, in a confidential undertone. "Nasty glitter in his eye. Hands all of a tremble. Better look out for him, sergeant. We don't want murder done. Well, anyhow, madam and gentlemen, what should you say if I was to tell you that we're able to retail that large bottle, as it stands—retail it, mind you—at three shillings and sixpence?"

"Three-and-six?" said Mr. Egg, surprised. "Why, I should have thought that wouldn't so much as pay the duty on the spirit."

"Nor it would," triumphed Mr. Redwood, "if it was spirit. But it isn't, and that's the whole point. It's a trade secret and I can't say more, but if you were to be asked whether that was or was not the finest Parma violet, equal to the most expensive marks, I don't mind betting you'd never know the difference."

"No, indeed," said Mr. Egg. "Wonderful, I call it. Pity they can't discover something similar to help the wine and spirit business, though I needn't say it wouldn't altogether do, or what would the Chancellor of the Exchequer have to say about it? Talking of that, what are you drinking? And you, miss? I hope you'll allow me, gentlemen. Same again all round, please."

The landlord hastened to fulfil the order and, as he passed through the bar-parlour, switched on the wireless, which instantly responded with the 9 o'clock time-signal, followed clearly by the voice of the announcer:

"This is the National programme from London. Before I read the weather report, here is a police message. In connection with the murder of Alice Steward, at Nottingham, we are asked by the Commissioner of Police to broadcast the following. The police are anxious to get in touch with a young man named Gerald Beeton, who is known to have visited the deceased on the afternoon preceding her death. This man is aged thirty-five, medium height, medium build, fair hair, small moustache, grey or blue eyes, full face, fresh colour. When last seen was wearing a grey lounge suit, soft grey hat and fawn overcoat, and is thought to be now travelling the country in a Morris car, number unknown. Will this man, or anyone able to throw light on his whereabouts, please communicate at once with the Superintendent of Police, Nottingham, or with any police-station? Here is the weather report. A deep depression . . ."

"Oh, switch it off, George," urged Mr. Redwood. "We don't want to hear about depressions."

"That's right," agreed the landlord, switching off. "What gets me is these police descriptions. How'd they think anyone's going to recognise a man from the sort of stuff they give you? Medium this and medium the other, and ordinary face and fair complexion and a soft hat—might be anybody."

"So it might," said Monty. "It might be me."

"Well, that's true, it might," said Mr. Redwood. "Or it might be this gentleman."

"That's a fact," admitted the man in the burberry. "Or it might be fifty men out of every hundred."

"Yes, or"—Monty jerked his head cautiously towards the newspaper in the corner—"him!"

"Well, so you say," said Redwood, "but nobody else has seen him to look at. Unless it's George."

"I wouldn't care to swear to him," said the landlord, with a smile. "He come straight in here and ordered a drink and paid for it without so much as looking at me, but from what I did see of him the description would fit him as well as anybody. And what's more, he's got a Morris car—it's in the garage now."

"That's nothing against him," said Monty. "So've I."

"And I," said the man in the burberry.

"And I," chimed in Redwood. "Encourage home industries, I say. But it's no help to identify a man. Beg your pardon, sergeant, and all that, but why don't the police make it a bit easier for the public?"

"Why," said the sergeant, "because they 'as to rely on the damnfool description given to them by the public. That's why."

"One up to you," said Redwood pleasantly. "Tell me, sergeant, all this stuff about wanting to interview the fellow is all eyewash, isn't it? I mean, what they really want to do is arrest him."

"That ain't for me to say," replied the sergeant ponderously. "You must use your own judgment about that. What they're asking for is an interview, him being known to have been one of the last people to see her before she was done in. If he's

101

sensible, he'll turn up. If he don't answer to the summons—well, you can think what you like."

"Who is he, anyway?" asked Monty.

"Now you want to know something. Ain't you seen the evening papers?"

"No; I've been on the road since five o'clock."

"Well, it's like this here. This old lady, Miss Alice Steward, lived all alone with a maid in a little 'ouse on the outskirts of Nottingham. Yesterday afternoon was the maid's afternoon out, and just as she was stepping out of the door, a bloke drives up in a Morris—or so *she* says, though you can't trust these girls, and if you ask me, it may just as well have been an Austin or Wolseley, or anything else, for that matter. He asks to see Miss Steward and the girl shows him into the sitting-room, and as she does so she hears the old girl say, 'Why, Gerald!'—like that. Well, she goes off to the pictures and leaves 'em to it, and when she gets back at 10 o'clock, she finds the old lady lying with 'er 'ead bashed in."

Mr. Redwood leaned across and nudged Mr. Egg. The stranger in the far corner had ceased to read his paper, and was peering stealthily round the edge of it.

"That's brought *him* to life, anyway," muttered Mr. Redwood. "Well, sergeant, but how did the girl know the fellow's surname and who he was?"

"Why," replied the sergeant, "she remembered once 'earing the old lady speak of a man called Gerald Beeton—a good many years ago, or so she said, and she couldn't tell us much about it. Only she remembered the name, because it was the same as the one on her cookery-book."

"Was that at Lewes?" demanded the young man called Arthur suddenly.

"Might have been," admitted the sergeant, glancing rather sharply at him. "The old lady came from Lewes. Why?"

"I remember, when I was a kid at school, hearing my mother mention an old Miss Steward at Lewes, who was very rich and had adopted a young fellow out of a chemist's shop. I think he ran away, and turned out badly, or something. Anyway, the old lady left the town. She was supposed to be very rich and to keep all her money in a tin box, or something.

My mother's cousin knew an old girl who was Miss Steward's housekeeper—but I daresay it was all rot. Anyhow, that was about six or seven years ago, and I believe my mother's cousin is dead now and the housekeeper too. My mother," went on the young man called Arthur, anticipating the next question, "died two years ago."

"That's very interesting, all the same," said Mr. Egg encouragingly. "You ought to tell the police about it."

"Well, I have, haven't I?" said Arthur, with a grin, indicating the sergeant. "Though I expect they know it already. Or do I have to go to the police-station?"

"For the present purpose," replied the sergeant, "I am a police-station. But you might give me your name and address."

The young man gave his name as Arthur Bunce, with an address in London. At this point the girl Gertrude was struck with an idea.

"But what about the tin box? D'you think he killed her to get it?"

"There's been nothing in the papers about the tin box," put in the man in the burberry.

"They don't let everything get into the papers," said the sergeant.

"It doesn't seem to be in the paper our disagreeable friend is reading," murmured Mr. Redwood, and as he spoke, that person rose from his seat and came over to the serving-hatch, ostensibly to order more beer, but with the evident intention of overhearing more of the conversation.

"I wonder if they'll catch the fellow," pursued Redwood thoughtfully. "They—by Jove! yes, that explains it—they must be keeping a pretty sharp look-out. I wondered why they held me up outside Wintonbury to examine my driving-licence. I suppose they're checking all the Morrises on the roads. Some job."

"All the Morrises in this district, anyway," said Monty. "They held me up just outside Thugford."

"Oho!" cried Arthur Bunce, "that looks as though they've got a line on the fellow. Now, sergeant, come across with it. What do you know about this, eh?"

"I can't tell you anything about that," replied Sergeant

Jukes, in a stately manner. The disagreeable man moved away from the serving-hatch, and at the same moment the sergeant rose and walked over to a distant table to knock out his pipe, rather unnecessarily, into a flowerpot. He remained there, refilling the pipe from his pouch, his bulky form towering between the Disagreeable Man and the door.

"They'll never catch him," said the Disagreeable Man, suddenly and unexpectedly. "They'll never catch him. And do you know why? I'll tell you. Not because he's too clever for them, but because he's too stupid. It's all too ordinary. I don't suppose it was this man Beeton at all. Don't you read your papers? Didn't you see that the old lady's sitting-room was on the ground floor, and that the dining-room window was found open at the top? It would be the easiest thing in the world for a man to slip in through the dining-room—Miss Steward was rather deaf—and catch her unawares and bash her on the head. There's only crazy paving between the garden gate and the windows, and there was a black frost yesterday night, so he'd leave no footmarks on the carpet. That's the difficult sort of murder to trace—no subtlety, no apparent motive. Look at the Reading murder, look at—"

"Hold hard a minute, sir," interrupted the sergeant. "How do you know there was crazy paving? *That's* not in the papers, as far as I know."

The Disagreeable Man stopped short in the full tide of his eloquence, and appeared disconcerted.

"I've seen the place, as a matter of fact," he said with some reluctance. "Went there this morning to look at it—for private reasons, which I needn't trouble you with."

"That's a funny thing to do, sir."

"It may be, but it's no business of yours."

"Oh, no, sir, of course not," said the sergeant. "We all of us has our little 'obbies, and crazy paving may be yours. Landscape gardener, sir?"

"Not exactly."

"A journalist, perhaps?" suggested Mr. Redwood.

"That's nearer," said the other. "Looking at my three fountain-pens, eh? Quite the amateur detective."

"The gentleman can't be a journalist," said Mr. Egg. "You

will pardon me, sir, but a journalist couldn't help but take an interest in Mr. Redwood's synthetic alcohol or whatever it is. I fancy I might put a name to your profession if I was called upon to do so. Every man carries the marks of his trade, though it's not always as conspicuous as Mr. Redwood's sample case or mine. Take books, for instance. I always know an academic gentleman by the way he opens a book. It's in his blood, as you might say. Or take bottles. I handle them one way—it's my trade. A doctor or a chemist handles them another way. This scent-bottle, for example. If you or I was to take the stopper out of this bottle, how would we do it? How would you do it, Mr. Redwood?"

"Me?" said Mr. Redwood. "Why, dash it all! On the word 'one' I'd apply the thumb and two fingers of the right hand *to* the stopper and on the word 'two' I would elevate them briskly, retaining a firm grip on the bottle with the left hand in case of accident. What would you do?" He turned to the man in the burberry.

"Same as you," said that gentleman, suiting the action to the word. "I don't see any difficulty about that. There's only one way I know of to take out stoppers, and that's to take 'em out. What d'you expect me to do? Whistle 'em out?"

"But this gentleman's quite right, all the same," put in the Disagreeable Man. "You do it that way because you aren't accustomed to measuring and pouring with one hand while the other's occupied. But a doctor or a chemist pulls the stopper out with his little finger, like this, and lifts the bottle in the same hand, holding the measuring-glass in his left—so—and when he—"

"Hi! Beeton!" cried Mr. Egg in a shrill voice, "look out!"

The flask slipped from the hand of the Disagreeable Man and crashed on the table's edge as the man in the burberry started to his feet. An overpowering odour of violets filled the room. The sergeant darted forward—there was a brief but violent struggle. The girl screamed. The landlord rushed in from the bar, and a crowd of men surged in after him and blocked the doorway.

"There," said the sergeant, emerging a little breathless from the mix-up, "you best come quiet. Wait a minute! Gotter charge you. Gerald Beeton, I arrest you for the murder of Alice Steward—stand still, can't you?—and I warns you as anything you say may be taken down and used in evidence at your trial. Thank you, sir. If you'll give me a 'and with him to the door, I've got a pal waiting just up the road, with a police car."

In a few minutes' time Sergeant Jukes returned, struggling into his overcoat. His amateur helpers accompanied him, their faces bright, as of those who have done their good deed for the day.

"That was a very neat dodge of yours, sir," said the sergeant, addressing Mr. Egg, who was administering a stiff pick-me-up to the young lady, while Mr. Redwood and the landlord together sought to remove the drench of Parma violet from the carpet. "Whew! Smells a bit strong, don't it? Regular barber's shop. We had the office he was expected this way, and I had an idea that one of you gentlemen might be the man, but I didn't know which. Mr. Bunce here saying that Beeton had been a chemist was a big help; and you, sir, I must say you touched him off proper."

"Not at all," said Mr. Egg. "I noticed the way he took that stopper out the first time—it showed he had been trained to laboratory work. That might have been an accident, of course. But afterwards, when he pretended he didn't know the right way to do it, I thought it was time to see if he'd answer to his name."

"Good wheeze," said the Disagreeable Man agreeably. "Mind if I use it some time?"

"Ah!" said Sergeant Jukes. "You gave me a bit of a turn, sir, with that crazy paving. Whatever did you—"

"Professional curiosity," said the other, with a grin. "I write detective stories. But our friend Mr. Egg is a better hand at the real thing."

"No, no," said Monty. "We all helped. The hardest problem's easy of solution when each one makes his little contribution. Isn't that so, Mr. Faggott?"

The aged countryman had risen to his feet.

"Place fair stinks o' that dratted stuff," he said disapprovingly. "I can't abide such nastiness." He hobbled out and shut the door.

CHAPTER III

◆

Murder in the Morning

"Half a mile along the main road to Ditchley, and then turn off to the left at the sign-post," said the Traveller in Mangles; "but I think you'll be wasting your time."

"Oh, well," said Mr. Montague Egg cheerfully, "I'll have a shot at the old bird. As the *Salesman's Handbook* says: 'Don't let the smallest chance slip by; you never know until you try.' After all, he's supposed to be rich, isn't he?"

"Mattresses stuffed with gold sovereigns, or so the neighbours say," acknowledged the Traveller in Mangles with a grin. "But they'd say anything."

"Thought you said there weren't any neighbours."

"No more they are. Manner of speaking. Well, good luck to it!"

Mr. Egg acknowledged the courtesy with a wave of his smart trilby, and let his clutch in with quiet determination.

The main road was thronged with the usual traffic of a Saturday morning in June—worthy holiday-makers bound for Melbury Woods or for the seashore about Beachampton—but as soon as he turned into the little narrow lane by the sign-post which said "Hatchford Mill 2 Miles," he was plunged into a profound solitude and silence, broken only by the scurry of an occasional rabbit from the hedgerow and the chug of his own Morris. Whatever else the mysterious Mr. Pinchbeck might be, he certainly was a solitary soul, and when, about a mile and a half down the lane, Monty caught sight of the tiny cottage, set far back in the middle of a neglected-looking field, he began to think that the Traveller in Mangles had been right. Rich though he might be, Mr. Pinchbeck was probably not a very likely customer for the wines and spirits supplied by Messrs. Plummet & Rose of Piccadilly. But, remembering Maxim Five of the *Salesman's Handbook*, "If you're a salesman worth the name at all, you can sell razors to a billiard-ball," Mr. Egg stopped his car at the entrance to the field, lifted the sagging gate and dragged it open, creaking in every rotten rail, and drove forward over the rough track, scarred with the ruts left by wet-weather traffic.

The cottage door was shut. Monty beat a cheerful tattoo upon its blistered surface, and was not very much surprised to get no answer. He knocked again, and then, unwilling to abandon his quest now he had come so far, walked round to the back. Here again he got no answer. Was Mr. Pinchbeck out? It was said that he never went out. Being by nature persistent and inquisitive, Mr. Egg stepped up to the window and looked in. What he saw made him whistle softly. He returned to the back door, pushed it open and entered.

When you arrive at a person's house with no intention beyond selling him a case of whisky or a dozen or so of port, it is disconcerting to find him stretched on his own kitchen floor, with his head battered to pulp. Mr. Egg had served two years on the Western Front, but he did not like what he saw. He put the table-cloth over it. Then, being a methodical sort of person, he looked at his watch, which marked 10.25. After a minute's pause for consideration, he made a rapid tour of the premises, then set off, driving as fast as he could, to fetch the police.

The inquest upon Mr. Humphrey Pinchbeck took place the following day, and resulted in a verdict of wilful murder against some person or persons unknown. During the next fortnight, Mr. Montague Egg, with some uneasiness, watched the newspapers. The police were following up a clue. A man was requested to communicate with the police. The man was described—a striking-looking person with a red beard and a check suit, driving a sports car with the registered number WOE 1313. The man was found. The man was charged and Mr. Montague Egg, three hundred miles away, was informed, to his disgust, that he would be required to give evidence before the magistrates at Beachampton.

The accused, who gave his name as Theodore Barton, age

forty-two, profession poet (at which Monty stared very hard, never having seen a poet at such close quarters), was a tall, powerfully built man, dressed in flamboyant tweeds, and having a certain air of rather disreputable magnificence about him. One would expect, thought Monty, to find him hanging about bars in the East Central district of London. His eyes were bold, and the upper part of his face handsome in its way; the mouth was hidden by the abundance of his tawny beard. He appeared to be perfectly at his ease, and was represented by a solicitor.

Montague Egg was called at an early stage to give evidence of the finding of the body. He mentioned that the time was 10:25 a.m. on Saturday, June 18th, and that the body was still quite warm when he saw it. The front door was locked; the back door shut, but not locked. The kitchen was greatly disordered, as though there had been a violent struggle, and a blood-stained poker lay beside the dead man. He had made a rapid search before sending for the police. In a bedroom upstairs he had seen a heavy iron box standing open and empty, with the keys hanging from the lock. There was no other person in the cottage, nor yet concealed about the little yard, but there were marks as though a large car had recently stood in a shed at the back of the house. In the sitting-room were the remains of breakfast for two persons. He (Mr. Egg) had passed down the lane from the high-road in his car, and had met nobody at all on the way. He had spent perhaps five or ten minutes in searching the place, and had then driven back by the way he came.

At this point Detective-Inspector Ramage explained that the lane leading to the cottage ran on for half a mile or so to pass Hatchford Mill, and then bent back to enter the main Beachampton road again at a point three miles nearer Ditchley.

The next witness was a baker named Bowles. He gave evidence that he had called at the cottage with his van at 10:15, to deliver two loaves of bread. He had gone to the back door, which had been opened by Mr. Pinchbeck in person. The old gentleman had appeared to be in perfect health, but a little flurried and irritable. He had not seen any other person in the kitchen, but had an impression that before he knocked he had heard two men's voices talking loudly and excitedly. The lad who had accompanied Bowles on his round confirmed this, adding that he fancied he had seen the outline of a man move across the kitchen window.

Mrs. Chapman, from Hatchford Mill, then came forward to say that she was accustomed to go in every week-day to Mr. Pinchbeck's cottage to do a bit of cleaning. She arrived at 7:30 and left at 9 o'clock. On Saturday 18th she had come as usual, to find that a visitor had arrived unexpectedly the night before. She identified the accused, Theodore Barton, as that visitor. He had apparently slept on the couch in the sitting-room, and was departing again that morning. She saw his car in the shed; it was a little sports one, and she had particularly noticed the number, WOE 1313, thinking that there was an unlucky number and no mistake. The interior of the shed was not visible from the back door. She had set breakfast for the two of them. The milkman and the postman had called before she left, and the grocer's van must have come soon after, for it was down at the Mill by 9:30. Nobody else ever called at the cottage, so far as she knew. Mr. Pinchbeck was a vegetarian and grew his own garden-stuff. She had never known him have a visitor before. She had heard nothing in the nature of "words" between Mr. Pinchbeck and the accused, but had thought the old man was not in the best of spirits. "He seemed a bit put out, like."

Then came another witness from the Mill, who had heard a car with a powerful engine drive very rapidly past the Mill a little before half-past ten. He had run out to look, fast cars being a rarity in the lane, but had seen nothing, on account of the trees which bordered the road at the corner just beyond the Mill.

At this point the police put in a statement made by the accused on his arrest. He said that he was the nephew of the deceased, and frankly admitted that he had spent the night at the cottage. Deceased had seemed pleased to see him, as they had not met for some time. On hearing that his nephew was "rather hard up," deceased had remonstrated with him about following so ill paid a profession as poetry, but had kindly offered him a small loan, which he, the accused, had gratefully accepted. Mr. Pinchbeck had then opened the box in his bed-room and brought out a number of banknotes, of which he had handed over "ten fivers," accompanying the gift by a little sermon on hard work and thrift. This had happened at about 9:45 or a little earlier—at any rate, after Mrs. Chapman was safely off the premises. The box had appeared to be full of banknotes and securities, and Mr. Pinchbeck had expressed distrust both of Mrs. Chapman and of the tradesmen in general. (Here Mrs. Chapman voiced an indignant protest, and had to be soothed by the Bench.) The statement went on to say that the accused had had no sort of quarrel with his uncle, and had left the cottage at, he thought, 10 o'clock or thereabouts, and driven on through Ditchley and Frogthorpe to Beachampton. There he had left his car with a friend, to whom it belonged, and had hired a motorboat and gone over to spend a fortnight in Brittany. Here he had heard nothing about his uncle's death till the arrival of Detective-Inspector Ramage had informed him of the suspicion against him. He had, of course, hastened back immediately to establish his innocence.

The police theory was that, as soon as the last tradesman had left the house, Barton had killed the old man, taken his keys, stolen the money, and escaped, supposing that the body would not be found till Mrs. Chapman arrived on the Monday morning.

While Theodore Barton's solicitor was extracting from Inspector Ramage the admission that the only money found on the accused at the time of his arrest was six Bank of England five-pound notes and a few shillings' worth of French money, Mr. Egg became aware that somebody was breathing very hard and excitedly down the back of his neck, and, on turning round, found himself face to face with an elderly woman, whose rather prominent eyes seemed ready to pop out of her head with agitation.

"Oh!" said the woman, bouncing in her seat. "Oh, dear!"

"I beg your pardon," said Mr. Egg, ever courteous. "Am I in your way, or anything?"

"Oh! oh, thank you! Oh, do tell me what I ought to do. There's something I ought to tell them. Poor man. He isn't guilty at all. I *know* he isn't. Oh, please do tell me what I ought to do. Do I have to go to the police? Oh, dear, oh, dear! I thought—I didn't know—I've never been in a place like this before! Oh, I know they'll bring him in guilty. Please, *please* stop them!"

"They can't bring him in guilty in this court," said Monty soothingly. "They can send him up for trial—"

"Oh, but they mustn't! He didn't do it. He wasn't there. Oh, please do something about it."

She appeared so earnest that Mr. Egg, slightly clearing his throat and settling his tie, rose boldly to his feet and exclaimed in stentorian accents: "Your Worship!"

The bench stared. The solicitor stared. The accused stared. Everybody stared.

"There is a lady here," said Monty, feeling that he must go through with it, "who tells me she has important evidence to give on behalf of the accused."

The staring eyes became focused upon the lady, who instantly started up, dropping her handbag, and crying: "Oh, dear! I'm so sorry! I'm afraid I ought to have gone to the police."

The solicitor, in whose face surprise, annoyance and anticipation struggled curiously together, at once came forward. The lady was extricated and a short whispered consultation followed, after which the solicitor said:

"Your worship, my client's instructions were to reserve his defence, but, since the lady, whom I have never seen until this moment, has so generously come forward with her statement, which appears to be a complete answer to the charge, perhaps your worship would prefer to hear her at this stage."

After a little discussion, the Bench decided that they would like to hear the evidence, if the accused was agreeable. Accordingly, the lady was put in the box, and sworn, in the name of Millicent Adela Queek.

"I am a spinster, and employed as art mistress at Woodbury High School for Girls. Saturday 18th was a holiday, of course, and I thought I would have a little picnic, all by my lonesome, in Melbury Woods. I started off in my own little car just about 9:30. It would take me about half an hour to get to Ditchley—I never drive very fast, and there was a lot of traffic on the road—most dangerous. When I got to Ditchley, I turned to the right, along the main road to Beachampton. After a little time I began to wonder whether I had put in quite enough petrol. My gauge isn't very reliable, you know, so I thought I'd better stop and make *quite* certain. So I pulled up at a roadside garage. I don't know *exactly* where it was, but it was quite a little way beyond Ditchley—between that and Helpington. It was one of those *dreadfully* ugly places, made of corrugated iron painted bright red. I don't think they should allow them to put up things like that. I asked the man there— a most obliging young man—to fill my tank, and while I was there I saw this gentleman—yes, I mean Mr. Barton, the accused—drive up in his dar. He was coming from the Ditchley direction and driving rather fast. He pulled up on the left-hand side of the road. The garage is on the right, but I saw him very distinctly. I couldn't mistake him—his beard, you know, and the clothes he was wearing—so distinctive. It was the same suit he is wearing now. Besides, I noticed the number of his car. Such a curious one, is it not? WOE 1313. Yes. Well, he opened the bonnet and did something to his plugs, I think, and then he drove on."

"What time was this?"

"I was just going to tell you. When I came to look at my watch I found it had stopped. Most vexatious. I think it was due to the vibration of the steering-wheel. But I looked up at the garage clock—there was one just over the door—and it said 10:20. So I set my watch by that. Then I went on to Melbury Woods and had my little picnic. So fortunate, wasn't it? that I looked at the clock then. Because my watch stopped again later on. But I do *know* that it was 10:20 when this gentleman stopped at the garage, so I don't see how he could have been doing a murder at that poor man's cottage between 10:15 and 10:25, because it must be well over twenty miles away—more, I should think."

Miss Queek ended her statement with a little gasp, and looked round triumphantly.

Detective-Inspector Ramage's face was a study. Miss Queek went on to explain why she had not come forward earlier with her story.

"When I read the description in the papers I thought it *must* be the same car I had seen, because of the number— but of course I couldn't be sure it was the same man, could

113

I? Descriptions are *so* misleading. And naturally I didn't want to be mixed up with a police case. The school, you know—parents don't like it. But I thought, if I came and saw this gentleman for myself, then I should be quite certain. And Miss Wagstaffe—our head-mistress—so kindly gave me leave to come, though to-day is very inconvenient, being my busiest afternoon. But I said it might be a matter of life and death, and so it is, isn't it?"

The magistrate thanked Miss Queek for her public-spirited intervention, and then, at the urgent request of both parties, adjourned the court for further inquiry into the new evidence.

Since it was extremely important that Miss Queek should identify the garage in question as soon as possible, it was arranged that she should set out at once in search of it, accompanied by Inspector Ramage and his sergeant, Mr. Barton's solicitor going with them to see fair play for his client. A slight difficulty arose, however. It appeared that the police car was not quite big enough to take the whole party comfortably, and Mr. Montague Egg, climbing into his own Morris, found himself hailed by the inspector with the request for a lift.

"By all means," said Monty; "a pleasure. Besides, you'll be able to keep your eye on me. Because, if that chap didn't do it, it looks to me as though I must be the guilty party."

"I wouldn't say that, sir," said the inspector, obviously taken aback by this bit of thought-reading.

"I couldn't blame you if you did," said Monty. He smiled, remembering his favourite motto for salesmen: "A cheerful voice and cheerful look puts orders in the order-book," and buzzed merrily away in the wake of the police car along the road from Beachampton to Ditchley.

"We ought to be getting near it now," remarked Ramage when they had left Helpington behind them. "We're ten miles from Ditchley and about twenty-five from Pinchbeck's cottage. Let's see—it'll be the left-hand side of the road, going in this direction. Hullo! this looks rather like it," he added presently. "They're pulling up."

The police car had stopped before an ugly corrugated-iron structure, standing rather isolated on the near side of the road, and adorned with a miscellaneous collection of enamelled advertisement-boards and a lot of petrol pumps. Mr Egg brought the Morris alongside.

"Is this the place, Miss Queek?"

"Well, I don't know. It was like this, and it was about here. But I can't be sure. All these dreadful little places are so much alike, but— Well, there! how stupid of me! Of course this isn't it. There's no clock. There ought to be a clock just over the door. So sorry to have made such a silly mistake. We must go on a little farther. It must be quite near here."

The little procession moved forward again, and five miles farther on came once more to a halt. This time there could surely be no mistake. Another hideous red corrugated garage, more boards, more petrol-pumps, and a clock, whose hands pointed (correctly, as the inspector ascertained by reference to his watch) to 7:15.

"I'm sure this must be it," said Miss Queek. "Yes—I recognise the man," she added, as the garage proprietor came out to see what was wanted.

The proprietor, when questioned, was not able to swear with any certainty to having filled Miss Queek's tank on June 18th. He had filled so many tanks before and since. But in the matter of the clock he was definite. It kept, and always had kept, perfect time, and it had never stopped or been out of order since it was first installed. If his clock had pointed to 10:20, then 10:20 was the time, and he would testify as much in any court in the kingdom. He could not remember having seen the car with the registered number WOE 1313, but there was no reason why he should, since it had not come in for attention. Motorists who wanted to do a spot of inspection often pulled up near his garage, in case they should find some trouble that needed expert assistance, but such incidents were so usual that he would pay no heed to them, especially on a busy morning.

Miss Queek, however, felt quite certain. She recognized the man, the garage and the clock. As a further precaution, the party went on as far as Ditchley, but, though the roadside was peppered the whole way with garages, there was no other exactly corresponding to the description. Either they were the wrong colour, or built of the wrong materials, or they had no clock.

"Well," said the inspector, rather ruefully, "unless we can prove collusion (which doesn't seem likely, seeing the kind of woman she is), that washes that out. That garage where she saw Barton is eighteen miles from Pinchbeck's cottage, and since we know the old man was alive at 10:15, Barton can't have killed him—not unless he was averaging 200 miles an hour or so, which can't be done yet awhile. Well, we've got to start all over again."

"It looks a bit awkward for me," said Monty pleasantly.

"I don't know about that. There's the voices that baker fellow heard in the kitchen. I know that couldn't have been you, because I've checked up your times." Mr. Ramage grinned. "Perhaps the rest of the money may turn up somewhere. It's all in the day's work. We'd better be getting back again."

Monty drove the first eighteen miles in thoughtful silence. They had just passed the garage with the clock (at which the inspector shook a mortified fist in passing), when Mr. Egg uttered an exclamation and pulled up.

"Hullo!" said the inspector.

"I've got an idea," said Monty. He pulled out a pocket-diary and consulted it. "Yes—I thought so. I've discovered a coincidence. Let's check up on it. Do you mind? 'Don't trust to luck, but be exact and verify the smallest fact.'" He replaced the diary and drove on, overhauling the police car. In process of time they came to the garage which had first attracted their attention—the one which conformed to specification, except in the particular that it displayed no clock. Here he stopped, and the police car, following in their tracks, stopped also.

The proprietor emerged expectantly, and the first thing that struck one about him was his resemblance to the man they had interviewed at the other garage. Monty commented politely on the fact.

"Quite right," said the man. "He's my brother."

"Your garages are alike, too," said Monty.

"Bought off the same firm," said the man. "Supplied in parts. Mass-production. Readily erected overnight by any handyman."

116

"That's the stuff," said Mr. Egg approvingly. "Standardisation means immense saving in labour, time, expense. You haven't got a clock, though."

"Not yet. I've got one on order."

"Never had one?"

"Never."

"Ever seen this lady before?"

The man looked Miss Queek carefully over from head to foot.

"Yes, I fancy I have. Came in one morning for petrol, didn't you, miss? Saturday fortnight or thereabouts. I've a good memory for faces."

"What time would that be?"

"Ten to eleven, or a few minutes after. I remember I was just boiling up a kettle for my elevenses. I generally take a cup of tea about then."

"Ten-fifty," said the inspector eagerly. "And this is—" he made a rapid calculation—"just on twenty-two miles from the cottage. Say half an hour from the time of the murder. Forty-four miles an hour—he could do that on his head in a fast sports car."

"Yes, but—" interrupted the solicitor.

"Just a minute," said Monty. "Didn't you," he went on, addressing the proprietor, "once have one of those clock-faces with movable hands to show lighting-up time?"

"Yes, I did. I've still got it, as a matter of fact. It used to hang over the door. But I took it down last Sunday. People found it rather a nuisance; they were always mistaking it for a real clock."

"And lighting-up time on June 18th," said Monty softly, "was 10:20, according to my diary."

"Well there," said Inspector Ramage, smiting his thigh. "Now, that's really clever of you, Mr. Egg."

"A brain-wave, a brain-wave," admitted Monty. "'The salesman who will use his brains will spare himself a world of pains'—or so the *Handbook* says."

CHAPTER IV

•

One Too Many

When Simon Grant, the Napoleon of Consolidated Nitro-Phosphates and Heaven knows how many affiliated companies, vanished off the face of the earth one rainy November night, it would have been, in any case, only natural that his family and friends should be disturbed, and that there should be a slight flurry on the Stock Exchange. But when, in the course of the next few days, it became painfully evident that Consolidated Nitro-Phosphates had been consolidated in nothing but the name—that they were, in fact, not even ripe for liquidation, but had (so to speak) already passed that point and evaporated into thin air, such assets as they possessed having mysteriously disappeared at the same time as Simon Grant—then the hue-and-cry went out with a noise that shook three continents and, incidentally, jogged Mr. Montague Egg for an hour or so out of his blameless routine.

Not that Mr. Egg had any money in Nitro-Phosphates, or could claim any sort of acquaintance with the missing financier. His connection with the case was entirely fortuitous, the by-product of a savage budgetary announcement by the Chancellor of the Exchequer, which threatened to have alarming results for the wine and spirits trade. Mr. Egg, travelling representative of Messrs. Plummet & Rose of Piccadilly, had reached Birmingham in his wanderings, when he was urgently summoned back to town by his employers for a special conference upon policy, and thus—though he did not know it at the time—he enjoyed the distinction of travelling by the very train from which Simon Grant so suddenly and unaccountably vanished.

The facts in the case of Simon Grant were disconcertingly simple. At this time the L.M.S. Railway were running a night express from Birmingham to London which, leaving Birmingham at 9:05, stopped only at Coventry and Rugby before running into Euston at 12:10. Mr. Grant had attended a dinner given in his honour by certain prominent business men in Coventry, and after dinner had had the unblushing effrontery to make a speech about the Prosperity of British Business. After this, he had hastened away to take the Birmingham express as far as Rugby, where he was engaged to stay the night with that pillar of financial rectitude, Lord Buddlethorp. He was seen into a first-class carriage at 9:57 by two eminently respectable Coventry magnates, who had remained chatting with him till the train started. There was one other person in his carriage— no less a man, in fact, than Sir Hicklebury Bowles, the well-known sporting baronet. In the course of conversation, he had mentioned to Sir Hicklebury (whom he knew slightly) that he was travelling alone, his secretary having succumbed to an attack of influenza. About half way between Coventry and Rugby, Mr. Grant had gone out into the corridor, muttering something about the heat. He had never been seen again.

At first, a very sinister light had been thrown on the incident by the fact that a door in the corridor, a little way up the train, had been found swinging open at Rugby, and the subsequent discovery of Mr. Grant's hat and overcoat a few miles farther up the line had led everybody to fear the worst. Careful examination, however, failed to produce either Simon Grant's corpse or any evidence of any heavy body having fallen from the train. In a pocket of the overcoat was a first-class ticket from Coventry to Rugby, and it seemed clear that, without this, he could not have passed the barrier at Rugby. Moreover, Lord Buddlethorp had sent his car with a chauffeur and a footman to meet the train at Rugby. The chauffeur had stood at the barrier and the footman had paraded the platform in search of the financier. Both knew him very well by sight, and between them they asserted positively that he had never left the train. Nobody had arrived at the barrier ticketless, or with the wrong ticket, and a check-up of the tickets issued for Rugby at Birmingham and Coventry revealed no discrepancy.

There remained two possibilities, both tempting and plausible. The Birmingham-London express reached Rugby at 10:24, departing again at 10:28. But, swift and impressive as it was, it was not the only, or the most important, pebble on the station beach, for over against it upon the down line was the Irish Mail, snorting and blowing in its three-minute halt before it roared away northwards at 10:25. If the express had been on time, Simon Grant might have slipped across and boarded it, and been at Holyhead by 2:25 to catch the steamer, and be in Dublin by 6:35, and Heaven only knew where a few hours after. As for the confident assertion of Lord Buddlethorp's footman, a trifling disguise—easily assumed in a lavatory or an empty compartment—would be amply sufficient to deceive him. To Chief Inspector Peacock, in charge of the investigations, the possibility appeared highly probable. It had also the advantage that the passengers crossing by the mailboat could be readily reckoned up and accounted for.

The question of tickets now became matter for inquiry. It was not likely that Simon Grant would have tried to secure them during his hasty one-minute dash for the Mail. Either he had taken them beforehand, or some accomplice had met him at Rugby and handed them over. Chief Inspector Peacock was elated when he discovered that tickets covering the train-and-streamer route from Rugby to Dublin had actually been purchased for the night in question from the L.M.S. agents in London in the absurd and incredible name of Solomon Grundy. Mr. Peacock was well acquainted with the feeble cunning which prompts people, when adopting an alias, to cling to their own initials. The underlying motive is, no doubt, a dread lest those same initials, inscribed on a watch, cigarette-case or what-not, should arouse suspicion, but the tendency is so well known that the choice of initials arouses in itself the very suspicion it is intended to allay. Mr. Peacock's hopes rose very high indeed when he discovered, in addition, that Solomon Grundy (Great Heavens, what a name!) had gone out of his way to give a fictitious and, indeed, non-existent address to the man at the ticket-office.

And then, just when the prospect seemed at its brightest, the whole theory received its death-blow. Not only had no Mr. Solomon Grundy travelled by the mailboat that night or any night—not only had his ticket never been presented or even cancelled—but it turned out to be impossible that Mr. Simon

Grant should have boarded the Irish Mail at all. For some tedious and infuriating reason connected with an overheated axle-box, the Birmingham-London express, on that night of all nights, had steamed into Rugby three minutes behind time and two minutes after the departure of the Mail. If this had been Simon Grant's plan of escape, something had undoubtedly gone wrong with it.

And, that being so, Chief Inspector Peacock came back to the old question: What had become of Simon Grant?

Talking it over with his colleagues, the Chief Inspector came eventually to the conclusion that Grant had, in fact, intended to take the Irish Mail, leaving the open door and the scattered garments behind him by way of confusing the trail for the police. What, then, would he do, when he found the Mail already gone? He could only leave the station and take another train. He had not left the station by the barrier, and careful inquiry convinced Mr. Peacock that it would have been extremely difficult for him to make his way out along the line unobserved, or hang about the railway premises till the following morning. An unfortunate suicide had taken place only the previous week, which had made the railwaymen particularly observant of stray passengers who might attempt to wander on to the permanent way; and, in addition, there happened to be two gangs of platelayers working with flares at points strategically placed for observation. So that Peacock, while not altogether dismissing this part of the investigation, turned it over as routine work to his subordinates, and bent his mind to consider a second main possibility that had already occurred to him before he had been led away by speculations on the Irish Mail.

This was, that Simon Grant had never left the express at all, but had gone straight through to Euston. London has great advantages as a hiding-place—and what better thing could Grant have done, when his first scheme failed him, than return to the express and continue his journey? His watch would have warned him, before he reached Rugby, that the Mail had probably left; a hasty inquiry and a quick dash to the booking-office, and he would be ready to continue his journey.

The only drawback was that when the Chief Inspector

questioned the officials in the booking-office he was met by the positive statement that no ticket of any kind had been issued that night later than 10:15. Nor yet had any passenger arrived at Euston minus a ticket. And the possibility of an accomplice on the platform had now to be dismissed, since the original plan of escape had not involved an accomplice, and it was not reasonable to suppose that one had been provided beforehand for such an emergency.

But, argued the Chief Inspector, the emergency might have been foreseen and a ticket purchased in advance. And if so, it was going to be extremely difficult to prove, since the number of tickets issued would correspond with the number of passengers. He set in train, however, an exhaustive investigation into the question of the tickets issued in London, Birmingham, Coventry and Rugby during the few weeks previous to the disappearance, thinking that he might easily light upon a return half which had come to hand very much subsequent to the date of issue, and that this might suggest a line of inquiry. In addition, he sent out a broadcast appeal, and this is where his line of inquiry impinged upon the orbit of Mr. Montague Egg.

"To the Chief Commissioner of Police.
—DEAR SIR,"

wrote Mr. Egg in his neat commercial hand,

"understanding as per the daily Press and the B.B.C. that you desire to receive communications from all persons travelling by the 9:05 p.m. Birmingham-London express on the 4th ult., I beg to inform you that I travelled by same (3rd class) from Coventry to Euston on the date mentioned and that I am entirely at your disposal for all enquiries. Being attached to the firm of Plummet & Rose, wine and spirit merchants, Piccadilly, as travelling representative, my permanent address will not find me at present, but I beg to enclose list of hotels where I shall be staying in the immediate future and remain, dear sir, yours faithfully."

In consequence of this letter, Mr. Egg was one evening mysteriously called out of the commercial room at the Cat and Fiddle in Oldham to speak with a Mr. Peacock.

"Pleased, I'm sure," said Mr. Egg, prepared for anything from a colossal order for wine and spirits to a forgotten acquaintance with a bad-luck story. "Monty-on-the-spot, that's me. What can I do for you, sir?"

Chief Inspector Peacock appeared to want every conceivable detail of information about Mr. Egg, his affairs and, in particular, his late journey to town. Monty disposed capably of the preliminaries and mentioned that he had arrived at the station with plenty of time to spare, and so had contrived to get a seat as soon as the train came in.

"And I was glad I did," he added. "I like to be comfortable, you know, and the train was rather crowded."

"I know it was crowded," said Mr. Peacock, with a groan. "And well I may, when I tell you that we have had to get in touch with every single person on that train, and interview as many of them as we could get hold of personally."

"Some job," said Mr. Egg, with the respect of one expert interviewer to another. "Do you mean you've got in touch with them all?"

"Every blessed one," said Mr. Peacock, "including several officious nuisances who weren't there at all, but hoped for a spot of notoriety."

"Talking of spots," said Monty, "what will you take?"

Mr. Peacock thanked him, and accepted a small whisky-and-soda. "Can you remember at all what part of the train you were in?"

"Certainly," said Mr. Egg promptly. "Third-class smoker, middle of the coach, middle of the train. Safest, you know, in case of accidents. Corner seat, corridor side, facing engine. Immediately opposite me, picture of York Minster, being visited by two ladies and a gentleman, in costumes of 1904 or thereabouts. Noticed it particularly, because everything else about the train was up to date. Thought it a pity."

"Hum," said Mr. Peacock. "Do you remember who else was in the compartment at Coventry?"

Monty screwed up his eyes as though to squeeze recollection out through his eyelids.

"Next me, stout, red, bald man, very sleepy, in tweeds. Been having one or two. He'd come from Birmingham. Next him, lanky young chap with pimples and a very bad bowler. Got in after me and tripped over my feet. Looked like a clerk. And a young sailor in the corner seat—there when I arrived. Talked all the time to the fellow in the corner opposite, who looked like some sort of a parson—collar round the wrong way, clerical hat, walrus moustache, dark spectacles, puffy cheeks and a tell-me-my-good-man way of talking. Next him—oh! yes, a fellow smoking a pipe of horrible scented sort of tobacco—might have been a small tradesman, but I didn't see much of him, because he was reading a paper most of the time. Then there was a nice, inoffensive, gentlemanly old bird who needed a hair-cut. He had pince-nez—very crooked— and never took his eyes off a learned-looking book. And opposite me there was a chap with a big brown beard in a yellow inverness cloak—foreign-looking—with a big, soft felt hat. He came from Birmingham, and so did the parson, but the other two on that side got in after I did."

The Chief Inspector smiled as he turned over the pages of a formidable bunch of documents. "You're an admirable witness, Mr. Egg. Your account tallies perfectly with those of your seven fellow-travellers, but it's the only one of the eight that's complete. You are obviously observant."

"My job," said Monty complacently.

"Of course. You may be interested to know that the gentlemanly old bird with the long hair was Professor Amblefoot of London University, the great authority of the Higher Calculus, and that he described you as a fair-haired, well-mannered young man."

"Much obliged to him, I'm sure," said Mr. Egg.

"The foreigner is Dr. Schleicher of Kew—resident there three years—the sailor and the parson we know all about— the drunk chap is O.K. too—we had his wife along, very voluble—the tradesman is a well-known Coventry resident, something to do with the Church Council of St. Michael's, and the pimply lad is one of Messrs. Morrison's clerks. They're all square. And they all went through to town, didn't they? Nobody left at Rugby?"

"Nobody," said Mr. Egg.

"Pity," said the Chief Inspector. "The truth is, Mr. Egg, that we can't hear of any person in the train who hasn't come forward and given an account of himself, and the number of people who have come forward precisely corresponds with the number of tickets collected at the barriers at Euston. You didn't observe any person continually hanging about the corridor, I suppose?"

"Not permanently," said Monty. "The chap with the beard got up and prowled a bit from time to time, I remember—seemed restless. I thought he perhaps didn't feel very well. But he'd only be absent a few minutes at a time. He seemed to be a nervous, unpleasant sort of chap—chewed his nails, you know, and muttered in German, but he—"

"Chewed his nails?"

"Yes. Very unpleasant, I must say. 'Well-kept hands that please the sight seize the trade and hold it tight, but bitten nails and grubby claws well may give the buyer pause.' So the *Salesman's Handbook* says,"—and Monty smirked gently at his own finger-tips. "This person's hands were—definitely not gentlemanly. Bitten to the quick."

"But that's really extraordinary," said Peacock. "Dr. Schleicher's hands are particularly well kept. I interviewed him myself yesterday. Surely he can't suddenly have abandoned the habit of nail-biting? People don't—not like that. And why should he? Was there anything else you noticed about the man opposite you?"

"I don't think so. Yes. Stop a moment. He smoked cigars at a most extraordinary rate. I remember his going out into the corridor with one smoked down to about an inch and coming back, five minutes afterwards, with a new one smoked half way through. Full-sized Coronas too—good ones; and I know quite a bit about cigars."

Peacock stared and then smote his hand lightly upon the table.

"I've got it!" he said. "I remember where I met a set of

125

badly chewed-up nails lately. By Jove! Yes, but how could he..."

Monty waited for enlightenment.

"Simon Grant's secretary. He was supposed to be in town all that day and evening, having 'flu—but how do I know that he was? But, even so, what good could he do by being in the train in disguise? And what could Dr. Schleicher have to do with it? It's Simon Grant we want—and Schleicher isn't Grant—at least"—the Chief Inspector paused and went on more dubiously—"I don't see how he could be. They know him well in the district, though he's said to be away from home a good deal, and he's got a wife—"

"Oh, has he?" said Mr. Egg, with a meaning emphasis.

"A double life, mean you?" said the Chief Inspector.

"And a double wife," said Mr. Egg. "You will pardon my asking a delicate question, but—er—are you certain you would spot a false beard at once, if you weren't altogether expecting it?"

"In a good light, I probably should, but by the light of the doctor's reading-lamp— But what's the game, Mr. Egg? If Schleicher is Grant, who was the man you saw in the train— the man with the bitten finger-nails? Grant doesn't bite his nails, I know that—he's rather particular about his appearance, so I'm told, though I've never met him myself."

"Well," said Mr. Egg, "since you ask me, why shouldn't the other man in the train be all three of them?"

"All three of which?"

"Grant and Schleicher and the secretary."

"I don't quite get you."

"Well, I mean—supposing Grant is Schleicher, with a nice ready-made personality all handy for him to step into, built up, as you may say, over the last three years, with money salted away in the name of Schleicher—well, I mean, there he is, as you might say, waiting to slip over to the Continent as soon as the fuss has died down—complete with unofficial lady."

"But the secretary?"

"The secretary was the man in train, made up as Grant

126

made up as Schleicher. I mean, speaking as a fool, I thought he might be."

"But where was Schleicher—I mean, Grant?"

"He was the man in the train, too. I mean, he may have been."

"Do you mean there were two of them?"

"Yes—at least, that's how I see it. You're the best judge, and I shouldn't like to put myself forward. But they'd be playing Box and Cox. Secretary gets in at Birmingham as Schleicher. Grant gets in at Coventry as Grant. Between Coventry and Rugby Grant changes to Schleicher in a wash-place or somewhere, and hangs about the platform and corridor till the train starts with him in it. He retires presently into a wash-place again. At a prearranged moment, secretary gets up, walks along the corridor and retires elsewhere, while Grant comes out and takes his place. Presently Grant walks down the corridor and secretary comes back to the compartment. They're never both visible at the same time, except for the two or three minutes while Grant is re-entering the train at Rugby, while honest witnesses like me are ready to come forward and swear that Schleicher got in at Birmingham, sat tight in his seat at Coventry and Rugby, and went straight through to Euston—as he did. I can't say I noticed any difference between the two Schleichers, except in the matter of the cigar. But they were very hairy and muffled up."

The Chief Inspector turned this over in his mind.

"Which of them was Schleicher when they got out at Euston?"

"Grant, surely. The secretary would remove his disguise at the last moment and emerge as himself, taking the thousand-to-one chance of somebody recognising him."

Peacock swore softly. "If that's what he did," he exclaimed, "we've got him on toast. Wait a moment, though. I *knew* there was a snag. If that's what they did, there ought to have been an extra third-class ticket at Euston. They can't both have travelled on one ticket."

"Why not?" said Mr. Egg. "I have often—at least, I don't exactly mean that, but I have from time to time laid a wager with an acquaintance that I would travel on his ticket, and got away with it."

"Perhaps," said Chief Inspector Peacock, "you would oblige me, sir, by outlining your method."

"Oh, certainly," said Mr. Egg. "'Speak the truth with cheerful ease if you would both convince and please'—Monty's favourite motto. If I had been Mr. Grant's secretary, I'd have taken a return ticket from Birmingham to London, and when the outward half had been inspected for the last time at Rugby, I'd pretend to put it in my pocket. But I wouldn't really. I'd shove it down at the edge of my seat and go for my stroll along the corridor. Then when Grant took my place—recognizing the right seat by an attaché-case, or something of that sort left on it—he'd retrieve the ticket and retain it. At the end of the journey, I'd slip off my beard and spectacles and so on, stick them in my overcoat pocket and fold the conspicuous overcoat inside-out and carry it on my arm. Then I'd wait to see Grant get out, and follow him up to the barrier, keeping a little way behind. He'd go through, giving up his ticket, and I'd follow along with a bunch of other people, making a little bustle and confusion in the gateway. The ticket-collector would stop me and say: 'I haven't got your ticket, sir.' I'd be indignant, and say: 'Oh, yes, you have.' He'd say: 'I don't think so, sir.' Then I'd protest, and he'd probably ask me to stand aside a minute while he dealt with the other passengers. Then I'd say: 'See here, my man, I'm quite sure I gave up my ticket. Look! Here's the return half, number so-and-so. Just look through your bunch and see if you haven't got the companion half.' He looks and he finds it, and says: 'I beg your pardon, sir; you're quite right. Here it is.' I say: 'Don't mention it,' and go through. And even if he suspects me, he can't prove anything, and the other fellow is well out of the way by that time."

"I see," said the Chief Inspector. "How often did you say you had indulged in this little game?"

"Well, never twice at the same station. It doesn't do to repeat one's effects too often."

"I think I'd better interview Schleicher and his secretary again," said Peacock pensively. "And the ticket-collector. I suppose we were meant to think that Grant had skipped to the

Irish Mail. I admit we should have thought so but for the accident that the Mail left before the London train came in. However, it takes a clever criminal to beat our organisation. By the way, Mr. Egg, I hope you will not make a habit—"

"Talking of bad habits," said Monty happily, "what about another spot?"

CHAPTER V

•

Murder at Pentecost

"Buzz off, Flathers," said the young man in flannels.

"We're thrilled by your news, but we don't want your religious opinions. And, for the Lord's sake, stop talking about 'undergrads,' like a ruddy commercial traveller. Hop it!"

The person addressed, a pimply youth in a commoner's gown, bleated a little, but withdrew from the table, intimidated.

"Appalling little tick," commented the young man in flannels to his companion. "He's on my staircase, too. Thank Heaven, I move out next term. I suppose it's true about the Master? Poor old blighter—I'm quite sorry I cut his lecture. Have some more coffee?"

"No, thanks, Radcott. I must be pushing off in a minute. It's getting too near lunch-time."

Mr. Montague Egg, seated at the next small table, had pricked up his ears. He now turned, with an apologetic cough, to the young man called Radcott.

"Excuse me, sir," he said, with some diffidence. "I didn't intend to overhear what you gentlemen were saying, but might I ask a question?" Emboldened by Radcott's expression, which, though surprised, was frank and friendly, he went on: "I happen to be a commercial traveller—Egg is my name, Montague Egg, representing Plummet & Rose, wines and spirits, Piccadilly. Might I ask what is wrong with saying 'undergrads'? Is the expression offensive in any way?"

Mr. Radcott blushed a fiery red to the roots of his flaxen hair.

"I'm frightfully sorry," he said ingenuously, and suddenly looking extremely young. "Damn stupid thing of me to say. Beastly brick."

"Don't mention it, I'm sure," said Monty.

"Didn't mean anything personal. Only, that chap Flathers gets my goat. He ought to know that nobody says 'undergrads' except townees and journalists and people outside the university."

"What ought we to say? 'Undergraduates'?"

"'Undergraduates' is correct."

"I'm very much obliged," said Monty. "Always willing to learn. It's easy to make a mistake in a thing like that, and, of course, it prejudices the customer against one. The *Salesman's Handbook* doesn't give any guidance about it; I shall have to make a memo for myself. Let me see. How would this do? 'To call an Oxford gent an—'"

"I think I should say 'Oxford man'—it's the more technical form of expression."

"Oh, yes. 'To call an Oxford man an undergrad proclaims you an outsider and a cad.' That's very easy to remember."

"You seem to have a turn for this kind of thing," said Radcott, amused.

"Well, I think perhaps I have," admitted Monty, with a touch of pride. "Would the same thing apply at Cambridge?"

"Certainly," replied Radcott's companion. "And you might add that 'To call the university the 'varsity is out of date, if not precisely narsity.' I apologise for the rhyme. 'Varsity has somehow a flavour of the 'nineties."

"So has the port I'm recommending," said Mr. Egg brightly. "Still, one's sales-talk must be up to date, naturally; and smart, though not vulgar. In the wine and spirit trade we make refinement our aim. I am really much obliged to you, gentlemen, for your help. This is my first visit to Oxford. Could you tell me where to find Pentecost College? I have a letter of introduction to a gentleman there."

"Pentecost?" said Radcott. "I don't think I'd start there, if I were you."

"No?" said Mr. Egg, suspecting some obscure point of university etiquette. "Why not?"

"Because," replied Radcott surprisingly, "I understand from the regrettable Flathers that some public benefactor has just murdered the Master, and in the circumstances I doubt whether the Bursar will be able to give proper attention to the merits of rival vintages."

"Murdered the Master?" echoed Mr. Egg.

"Socked him one—literally, I am told, with a brick-bat enclosed in a Woolworth sock—as he was returning to his house from delivering his too-well-known lecture on Plato's use of the Enclitics. The whole school of *Literae Humaniores* will naturally be under suspicion, but, personally, I believe Flathers did it himself. You may have heard him informing us that judgment overtakes the evil-doer, and inviting us to a meeting for prayer and repentance in the South Lecture-Room. Such men are dangerous."

"Was the Master of Pentecost an evil-doer?"

"He has written several learned works disproving the existence of Providence, and I must say that I, in common with the whole Pentecostal community, have always looked on him as one of Nature's worst mistakes. Still, to slay him more or less on his own doorstep seems to me to be in poor taste. It will upset the examination candidates, who face their ordeal next week. And it will mean cancelling the Commem. Ball. Besides, the police have been called in, and are certain to annoy the Senior Common Room by walking on the grass in the quad. However, what's done can't be undone. Let us pass to a pleasanter subject. I understand that you have some port to dispose of. I, on the other hand, have recently suffered bereavement at the hands of a bunch of rowing hearties, who invaded my rooms the other night and poured my last dozen of Cockburn '04 down their leathery and undiscriminating throttles. If you care to stroll round with me to Pentecost, Mr. Egg, bringing your literature with you, we might be able to do business."

Mr. Egg expressed himself as delighted to accept Radcott's invitation, and was soon trotting along the Cornmarket at his conductor's athletic heels. At the corner of Broad Street the second undergraduate left them, while they turned on, past Balliol and Trinity, asleep in the June sunshine, and presently reached the main entrance of Pentecost.

Just as they did so, a small, elderly man, wearing a light overcoat and carrying an M.A. gown over his arm, came ambling short-sightedly across the street from the direction of the Bodleian Library. A passing car just missed whirling him into eternity, as Radcott stretched out a long arm and raked him into safety on the pavement.

"Look out, Mr. Temple," said Radcott. "We shall be having *you* murdered next."

"Murdered?" queried Mr. Temple, blinking. "Oh, you refer to the motor-car. But I saw it coming. I saw it quite distinctly. Yes, yes. But why 'next'? Has anybody else been murdered?"

"Only the Master of Pentecost,' said Radcott, pinching Mr. Egg's arm.

"The Master? Dr. Greeby? You don't say so! Murdered? Dear me! Poor Greeby! This will upset my whole day's work." His pale-blue eyes shifted, and a curious, wavering look came into them. "Justice is slow but sure. Yes, yes. The sword of the Lord and of Gideon. But the blood—that is always so disconcerting, is it not? And yet, I washed my hands, you know." He stretched out both hands and looked at them in a puzzled way. "Ah, yes—poor Greeby has paid the price of his sins. Excuse my running away from you—I have urgent business at the police-station."

"If," said Mr. Radcott, again pinching Monty's arm, "you want to give yourself up for the murder, Mr. Temple, you had better come along with us. The police are bound to be about the place somewhere."

"Oh, yes, of course, so they are. Yes. Very thoughtful of you. That will save me a great deal of time, and I have an important chapter to finish. A beautiful day, is it not, Mr.—I fear I do not know your name. Or do I? I am growing sadly forgetful."

Radcott mentioned his name, and the oddly assorted trio turned together towards the main entrance to the college. The great gate was shut; at the postern stood the porter, and at his side a massive figure in blue, who demanded their names.

Radcott, having been duly identified by the porter, produced Monty and his credentials.

"And this," he went on, "is, of course, Mr. Temple. You know him. He is looking for your Superintendent."

"Right you are, sir," replied the policeman. "You'll find him in the cloisters. . . . At his own game, I suppose?" he added, as the small figure of Mr. Temple shuffled away across the sun-baked expanse of the quad.

"Oh, yes," said Radcott. "He was on to it like a shot. Must be quite exciting for the old bird to have a murder so near home. Where was his last?"

"Lincoln, sir; last Tuesday. Young fellow shot his young woman in the Cathedral. Mr. Temple was down at the station the next day, just before lunch, explaining that he'd done it because the poor girl was the Scarlet Woman."

"Mr. Temple," said Radcott, "has a mission in life. He is the sword of the Lord and of Gideon. Every time a murder is committed in this country, Mr. Temple lays claim to it. It is true that his body can always be shown to have been quietly in bed or at the Bodleian while the dirty work was afoot, but to an idealistic philosopher that need present no difficulty. But what *is* all this about the Master, actually?"

"Well, sir, you know that little entry between the cloisters and the Master's residence? At twenty minutes past ten this morning, Dr. Greeby was found lying dead there, with his lecture-notes scattered all round him and a brickbat in a woollen sock lying beside his head. He'd been lecturing in a room in the Main Quadrangle at nine o'clock, and was, as far as we can tell, the last to leave the lecture-room. A party of American ladies and gentlemen passed through the cloisters a little after 10 o'clock, and they have been found, and say there was nobody about there then, so far as they could see—but, of course, sir, the murderer might have been hanging about the entry, because, naturally, they wouldn't go that way but through Boniface Passage to the Inner Quad and the chapel. One of the young gentlemen says he saw the Master cross the Main Quad on his way to the cloisters at 10:05, so he'd reach the entry in about two minutes after that. The Regius Professor of Morphology came along at 10:20, and found the body, and when the doctor arrived, five minutes later, he said Dr. Greeby must have been dead about a quarter of an hour. So that puts it somewhere round about 10:10, you see, sir."

"When did these Americans leave the chapel?"

"Ah, there you are, sir!" replied the constable. He seemed very ready to talk, thought Mr. Egg, and deduced, rightly, that Mr. Radcott was well and favourably known to the Oxford branch of the Force. "If that there party had come back through the cloisters, they might have been able to tell us something. But they didn't. They went on through the Inner Quad into the garden, and the verger didn't leave the chapel, on account of a lady who had just arrived and wanted to look at the carving on the reredos."

"And did the lady also come through the cloisters?"

"She did, sir, and she's the person we want to find, because it seems as though she must have passed through the cloisters very close to the time of the murder. She came into the chapel just on 10:15, because the verger recollected of the clock chiming a few minutes after she came in and her mentioning how sweet the notes was. You see the lady come in, didn't you, Mr. Dabbs?"

"I saw *a* lady," replied the porter, "but then I see a lot of ladies one way and another. This one came across from the Bodleian round about 10 o'clock. Elderly lady, she was, dressed kind of old-fashioned, with her skirts round her heels and one of them hats like a rook's nest and a bit of elastic round the back. Looked like she might be a female don—leastways, the way female dons used to look. And she had the twitches—you know—jerked her head a bit. You get hundreds like 'em. They goes to sit in the cloisters and listen to the fountain and the little birds. But as to noticing a corpse or a murderer, it's my belief they wouldn't know such a thing if they saw it. I didn't see the lady again, so she must have gone out through the garden."

"Very likely," said Radcott. "May Mr. Egg and I go in through the cloisters, officer? Because it's the only way to my rooms, unless we go round by St. Scholastica's Gate."

"All the other gates are locked, sir. You go on and speak to the Super; he'll let you through. You'll find him in the cloisters with Professor Staines and Dr. Moyle."

"Bodley's Librarian? What's he got to do with it?"

"They think he may know the lady, sir, if she's a Bodley reader."

"Oh, I see. Come along, Mr. Egg."

Radcott led the way across the Main Quadrangle and through a dark little passage at one corner, into the cool shade of the cloisters. Framed by the arcades of ancient stone, the green lawn drowsed tranquilly in the noonday heat. There was no sound but the echo of their own footsteps, the plash and tinkle of the little fountain and the subdued chirping of chaffinches, as they paced the alternate sunshine and shadow of the pavement. About midway along the north side of the cloisters they came upon another dim little covered passageway, at the entrance to which a police-sergeant was kneeling, examining the ground with the aid of an electric torch.

"Hullo, sergeant!" said Radcott. "Doing the Sherlock Holmes stunt? Show us the bloodstained footprints."

"No blood, sir, unfortunately. Might make our job easier if there were. And no footprints neither. The poor gentleman was sandbagged, and we think the murderer must have climbed up here to do it, for the deceased was a tall gentleman and he was hit right on the top of the head, sir." The sergeant indicated a little niche, like a blocked-up window, about four feet from the ground. "Looks as if he'd waited up here, sir, for Dr. Greeby to go by."

"He must have been well acquainted with his victim's habits," suggested Mr. Egg.

"Not a bit of it," retorted Radcott. "He'd only to look at the lecture-list to know the time and place. This passage leads to the Master's House and the Fellows' Garden and nowhere else, and it's the way Dr. Greeby would naturally go after his lecture, unless he was lecturing elsewhere, which he wasn't. Fairly able-bodied, your murderer, sergeant, to get up here. At least—I don't know."

Before the policeman could stop him, he had placed one

hand on the side of the niche and a foot on a projecting band of masonry below it, and swung himself up.

"Hi, sir! Come down, please. The Super won't like that."

"Why? Oh, gosh! Fingerprints, I suppose. I forgot. Never mind; you can take mine if you want them, for comparison. Give you practice. Anyhow, a baby in arms could get up here. Come on, Mr. Egg; we'd better beat it before I'm arrested for obstruction."

But at this moment Radcott was hailed by a worried-looking don, who came through the passage from the far side, accompanied by three or four other people.

"Oh, Mr. Radcott! One moment, Superintendent, this gentleman will be able to tell you what you want to know; he was at Dr. Greeby's lecture. That is so, is it not, Mr. Radcott?"

"Well, no, not exactly, sir," replied Radcott, with some embarrassment. "I should have been, but, by a regrettable accident, I cut—that is to say, I was on the river, sir, and didn't get back in time."

"Very vexatious," said Professor Staines, while the Superintendent merely observed:

"Any witness to your being on the river, sir?"

"None," replied Radcott. "I was alone in a canoe, up a backwater—earnestly studying Aristotle. But I really didn't murder the Master. His lectures were—if I may say so—dull, but not to that point exasperating."

"That is a very impudent observation, Mr. Radcott," said the Professor severely, "and in execrable taste."

The Superintendent, murmuring something about routine, took down in a note-book the alleged times of Mr. Radcott's departure and return, and then said:

"I don't think I need detain any of you gentlemen further. If we want to see you again, Mr. Temple, we will let you know."

"Certainly, certainly. I shall just have a sandwich at the café and return to the Bodleian. As for the lady, I can only repeat that she sat at my table from about half-past nine till just before ten, and returned again at ten-thirty. Very restless and disturbing. I do wish, Dr. Moyle, that some arrangement could be made to give me that table to myself, or that I could

136

be given a place apart in the library. Ladies are always restless and disturbing. She was still there when I left, but I very much hope she has now gone for good. You are sure you don't want to lock me up now? I am quite at your service."

"Not just yet, sir. You will hear from us presently."

"Thank you, thank you. I should like to finish my chapter. For the present, then, I will wish you good-day."

The little bent figure wandered away, and the Superintendent touched his head significantly.

"Poor gentleman! Quite harmless, of course. I needn't ask you, Dr. Moyle, where *he* was at the time?"

"Oh, he was in his usual corner of Duke Humphrey's Library. He admits it, you see, when he is asked. In any case, I know definitely that he was there this morning, because he took out a Phi book, and of course had to apply personally to me for it. He asked for it at 9:30 and returned it at 12:15. As regards the lady, I think I have seen her before. One of the older school of learned ladies, I fancy. If she is an outside reader, I must have her name and address somewhere, but she may, of course, be a member of the University. I fear I could not undertake to know them all by sight. But I will inquire. It is, in fact, quite possible that she is still in the library, and, if not, Franklin may know when she went and who she is. I will look into the matter immediately. I need not say, professor, how deeply I deplore this lamentable affair. Poor dear Greeby! Such a loss to classical scholarship!"

At this point, Radcott gently drew Mr. Egg away. A few yards farther down the cloisters, they turned into another and rather wider passage, which brought them out into the Inner Quadrangle, one side of which was occupied by the chapel. Mounting three dark flights of stone steps on the opposite side, they reached Radcott's rooms, where the undergraduate thrust his new acquaintance into an armchair, and, producing some bottles of beer from beneath the window-seat, besought him to make himself at home.

"Well," he observed presently, "you've had a fairly lively introduction to Oxford life—one murder and one madman. Poor old Temple. Quite one of our prize exhibits. Used to be a Fellow here, donkey's years ago. There was some fuss, and he disappeared for a time. Then he turned up again, ten years since, perfectly potty; took lodgings in Holywell, and has haunted the Bodder and the police-station alternately ever since. Fine Greek scholar he is, too. Quite reasonable, except on the one point. I hope old Moyle finds his mysterious lady, though it's nonsense to pretend that they keep tabs on all the people who use the library. You've only got to walk in firmly, as if the place belonged to you, and, if you're challenged, say in a loud, injured tone that you've been a reader for years. If you borrow a gown, they won't even challenge you."

"Is that so, really?" said Mr. Egg.

"Prove it, if you like. Take my gown, toddle across to the Bodder, march straight in past the showcases and through the little wicket marked 'Readers Only,' into duke Humphrey's Library; do what you like, short of stealing the books or setting fire to the place—and if anybody says anything to you, I'll order six dozen of anything you like. That's fair, isn't it?"

Mr. Egg accepted this offer with alacrity, and in a few moments, arrayed in a scholar's gown, was climbing the stair that leads to England's most famous library. With a slight tremor, he pushed open the swinging glass door and plunged into the hallowed atmosphere of mouldering leather that distinguishes such temples of learning.

Just inside, he came upon Dr. Moyle in conversation with the door-keeper. Mr. Egg, bending nonchalantly to examine an illegible manuscript in a showcase, had little difficulty in hearing what they said, since, like all official attendants upon reading-rooms, they took no trouble to lower their voices.

"I know the lady, Dr. Moyle. That is to say, she has been here several times lately. She usually wears an M.A. gown. I saw her here this morning, but I didn't notice when she left. I don't think I ever heard her name, but seeing that she was a senior member of the University—"

Mr. Egg waited to hear no more. An idea was burgeoning in his mind. He walked away, courageously pushed open the Readers' Wicket, and stalked down the solemn mediaeval length of Duke Humphrey's Library. In the remotest and darkest bay, he observed Mr. Temple, who, having apparently had his sandwich and forgotten about the murder, sat alone, writing busily, amid a pile of repellent volumes, with a large attaché-case full of papers open before him.

Leaning over the table, Mr. Egg addressed him in an urgent whisper:

"Excuse me, sir. The police Superintendent asked me to say that they think they have found the lady, and would be glad if you would kindly step down at once and identify her."

"The lady?" Mr. Temple looked up vaguely. "Oh, yes— the lady. To be sure. Immediately? That is not very convenient. Is it so very urgent?"

"They said particularly to lose no time, sir," said Mr. Egg.

Mr. Temple muttered something, rose, seemed to hesitate whether to clear up his papers or nor, and finally shovelled them all into the bulging attaché-case, which he locked upon them.

"Let me carry this for you, sir," said Monty, seizing it promptly and shepherding Mr. Temple briskly out. "They're still in the cloisters, I think, but the Super said, would you kindly wait a few moments for him in the porter's lodge. Here we are."

He handed Mr. Temple and his attaché-case over to the care of the porter, who looked a little surprised at seeing Mr. Egg in academic dress, but, on hearing the Superintendent's name, said nothing. Mr. Egg hastened through quad and cloisters and mounted Mr. Radcott's staircase at a run.

"Excuse me, sir," he demanded breathlessly of that young gentleman, "but what is a Phi book?"

"A Phi book," replied Radcott, in some surprise, "is a book deemed by Bodley's Librarian to be of an indelicate nature, and catalogued accordingly, by some dead-and-gone humorist, under the Greek letter *phi*. Why the question?"

"Well," said Mr. Egg, "it just occurred to me how simple it would be for anybody to walk into the Bodleian, disguise himself in a retired corner—say in Duke Humphrey's Library—walk out, commit a murder, return, change back to his own clothes and walk out. Nobody would stop a person from coming in again, if he—or she—had previously been seen to go out—especially if the disguise had been used in the library before. Just a change of clothes and an M.A. gown would be enough."

"What in the world are you getting at?"

"This lady, who was in the cloisters at the time of the murder. Mr. Temple says she was sitting at his table. But isn't it funny that Mr. Temple should have drawn special attention to himself by asking for a Phi book, to-day of all days? If he was once a Fellow of this college, he'd know which way Dr. Greeby would go after his lecture; and he may have had a grudge against him on account of that old trouble, whatever it was. He'd know about the niche in the wall, too. And he's got an attaché-case with him that might easily hold a lady's hat and a skirt long enough to hide his trousers. And why is he wearing a topcoat on such a hot day, if not to conceal the upper portion of his garments? Not that it's any business of mine—but—well, I just took the liberty of asking myself. And I've got him out there, with his case, and the porter keeping an eye on him."

Thus Mr. Egg, rather breathlessly. Radcott gaped at him.

"Temple? My dear man, you're as potty as he is. Why, he's always confessing—he confessed to this—you can't possibly suppose—"

"I daresay I'm wrong," said Mr. Egg. "But isn't there a fable about the man who cried 'Wolf!' so often that nobody would believe him when the wolf really came? There's a motto in the *Salesman's Handbook* that I always admire very much. It says: 'Discretion plays a major part in making up the salesman's art, for truths that no one can believe are calculated to deceive.' I think that's rather subtle, don't you?"

CHAPTER VI

◆

Maher-Shalal-Hashbaz

No Londoner can ever resist the attraction of a street crowd.
Mr. Montague Egg, driving up Kingsway, and observing a
group of people staring into the branches of one of the slender
plane-trees which embellish that thoroughfare, drew up to see
what all the excitement was about.

"Poor puss!" cried the bystanders, snapping encouraging
fingers. "Poor pussy, then! Kitty, kitty, kitty, come on!"

"Look, baby, look at the pretty pussy!"

"Fetch her a bit of cat's-meat."

"She'll come down when she's tired of it."

"Chuck a stone at her!"

"Now then, what's all this about?"

The slender, shabby child who stood so forlornly holding
the empty basket appealed to the policeman.

"Oh, do please send these people away! How *can* he come
down, with everybody shouting at him? He's frightened, poor
darling."

From among the swaying branches a pair of amber eyes
gleamed wrathfully down. The policeman scratched his head.

"Bit of a job, ain't it, missie? However did he come to get
up there?"

"The fastening came undone, and he jumped out of the
basket just as were getting off the 'bus. Oh, please do something!"

Mr. Montague Egg, casting his eye over the crowd, per-
ceived on its outskirts a window-cleaner with his ladders upon
a truck. He hailed him.

"Fetch that ladder along, sonnie, and we'll soon get him
down, if you'll allow me to try, miss. If we leave him to himself,
he'll probably stick up there for ages. 'It's hard to reassure,

persuade or charm the customer who once has felt alarm.' Carefully, now. That's the ticket."

"Oh, thank you so much! Oh, do be gentle with him. He does so hate being handled."

"That's all right, miss; don't you worry. Always the gentleman, that's Monty Egg. Kind about the house and clean with children. Up she goes!"

And Mr. Egg, clapping his smart trilby upon his head and uttering crooning noises, ascended into the leafage. A loud explosion of spitting sounds and a small shower of twigs floated down to the spectators, and presently Mr. Egg followed, rather awkwardly, clutching a reluctant bunch of ginger fur. The girl held out the basket, the four furiously kicking legs were somehow bundled in, a tradesman's lad produced a piece of string, the lid was secured, the window-cleaner was rewarded and removed his ladder, and the crowd dispersed. Mr. Egg, winding his pocket-handkerchief about a lacerated wrist, picked the scattered leaves out of his collar and straightened his tie.

"Oh, he's scratched you dreadfully!" lamented the girl, her blue eyes large and tragic.

"Not at all," replied Mr. Egg. "Very happy to have been of assistance, I am sure. Can I have the pleasure of driving you anywhere? It'll be pleasanter for him than a 'bus, and if we pull up the windows he can't jump out, even if he does get the basket open again."

The girl protested, but Mr. Egg firmly bustled her into his little saloon and inquired where she wanted to go.

"It's this address," said the girl, pulling a newspaper cutting out of her worn handbag. "Somewhere in Soho, isn't it?"

Mr. Egg, with some surprise, read the advertisement:

WANTED: hard-working, capable CAT (either sex), keep down mice in pleasant villa residence and be companion to middle-aged couple. Ten shillings and good home to suitable applicant. Apply personally to Mr. John Doe, La Cigale Bienheureuse, Frith St., W., on Tuesday between 11 and 1 o'clock.

"That's a funny set-out," said Mr. Egg, frowning.

"Oh! do you think there's anything wrong with it? Is it just a joke?"

"Well," said Mr. Egg, "I can't quite see why anybody wants to pay ten bob for an ordinary cat, can you? I mean, they usually come gratis and f.o.b. from somebody who doesn't like drowning kittens. And I don't quite believe in Mr. John Doe; he sounds like what they call a legal fiction."

"Oh dear!" cried the girl, with tears in the blue eyes. "I did so hope it would be all right. You see, we're so dreadfully hard up, with father out of work, and Maggie—that's my step-mother—says she won't keep Maher-shalal-hashbaz any longer, because he scratches the table-legs and eats as much as a Christian, bless him!—though he doesn't really—only a little milk and a bit of cat's-meat, and he's a beautiful mouser, only there aren't many mice where we live—and I thought, if I could get him a good home—and ten shillings for some new boots for Dad, he needs them so badly—"

"Oh, well, cheer up," said Mr. Egg. "Perhaps they're willing to pay for a full-grown, certified mouser. Or—tell you what—it may be one of these cinema stunts. We'll go and see, anyhow; only I think you'd better let me come with you and interview Mr. Doe. I'm quite respectable," he added hastily. "Here's my card. Montague Egg, travelling representative of Plummet & Rose, wines and spirits, Piccadilly. Interviewing customers is my long suit. 'The salesman's job is to get the trade—don't leave the house till the deal is made'—that's Monty's motto."

"My name's Jean Maitland, and Dad's in the commercial line himself—at least, he was till he got bronchitis last winter, and now he isn't strong enough to go on the road."

"Bad luck!" said Monty sympathetically, as he turned down High Holborn. He liked this child of sixteen or so, and registered a vow that "something should be done about it."

It seemed as though there were other people who thought ten shillings good payment for a cat. The pavement before the grubby little Soho restaurant was thick with cat-owners, some carrying baskets, some clutching their animals in their arms. The air resounded with the mournful cries of the prisoners.

"Some competition," said Monty. "Well, anyhow, the post doesn't seem to be filled yet. Hang on to me, and we'll try what we can do."

They waited for some time. It seemed that the applicants were being passed out through a back entrance, for, though many went in, some returned. Eventually they secured a place in the queue going up a dingy staircase, and, after a further eternity, found themselves facing a dark and discouraging door. Presently this was opened by a stout and pursy-faced man, with very sharp little eyes, who said briskly: "Next, please!" and they walked in.

"Mr. John Doe?" said Monty.

"Yes, Brought your cat? Oh, the young lady's cat. I see. Sit down, please. Name and address, miss?"

The girl gave an address south of the Thames, and the man made a note of it, "in case," he explained, "the chosen candidate should prove unsuitable, and I might want to write to you again. Now, let us see the cat."

The basket was opened, and a ginger head emerged resentfully.

"Oh, yes. Fine specimen. Poor pussy, then. He doesn't seem very friendly."

"He's frightened by the journey, but he's a darling when he once knows you, and a splendid mouser. And so clean."

"That's important. Must have him clean. And he must work for his living, you know."

"Oh, he will. He can tackle rats or anything. We call him Maher-shalal-hashbaz, because he 'makes haste to the spoil.' But he answers to Mash, don't you, darling?"

"I see. Well, he seems to be in good condition. No fleas? No diseases? My wife is very particular."

"Oh, no. He's a splendid healthy cat. Fleas, indeed!"

"No offence, but I must be particular, because we shall make a great pet of him. I don't care much for his colour. Ten shillings is a high price to pay for a ginger one. I don't know whether—"

"Come, come," said Monty. "Nothing was said in your advertisement about colour. This lady has come a long way to bring you the cat, and you can't expect her to take less than

144

she's offered. You'll never get a better cat than this; everyone knows that the ginger ones are the best mousers—they've got more go in them. And look at his handsome white shirt-front. It *shows* you how beautifully clean he is. And think of the advantage—you can *see* him—you and your good lady won't go tripping over him in a dark corner, same as you do with these black and tabby ones. As a matter of fact, we ought to charge extra for such a handsome colour as this. They're much rarer and more high-class than the ordinary cat."

"There's something in that," admitted Mr. Doe. "Well, look here, Miss Maitland. Suppose you bring Maher—what you said—out to our place this evening, and if my wife likes him we will keep him. Here's the address. And you must come at six precisely, please, as we shall be going out later."

Monty looked at the address, which was at the northern extremity of the Edgware-Morden Tube.

"It's a very long way to come on the chance," he said resolutely. "You will have to pay Miss Maitland's expenses."

"Oh, certainly," said Mr. Doe. "That's only fair. Here is half a crown. You can return me the change this evening. Very well, thank you. Your cat will have a really happy home if he comes to us. Put him back in his basket now. The other way out, please. Mind the step. *Good* morning."

Mr. Egg and his new friend, stumbling down an excessively confined and stuffy back staircase into a malodorous by-street, looked at one another.

"He seemed rather an abrupt sort of person," said Miss Maitland. "I do *hope* he'll be kind to Maher-shalal-hashbaz. You were *marvellous* about the gingeriness—I thought he was going to be stuffy about that. My angel Mash! how *anybody* could object to his beautiful colour!"

"Um!" said Mr. Egg. "Well, Mr. Doe may be O.K., but I shall believe in his ten shillings when I see it. And, in any case, you're not going to his house alone. I shall call for you in the car at five o'clock."

"But, Mr. Egg—I can't allow you! Besides, you've taken half a crown off him for my fare."

"That's only business," said Mr. Egg. "Five o'clock sharp I shall be there."

"Well, come at four, and let us give you a cup of tea, anyway. That's the least we can do."

"Pleased, I'm sure," said Mr. Egg.

The house occupied by Mr. Doe was a new detached villa standing solitary at the extreme end of a new and unmade suburban road. It was Mrs. Doe who answered the bell—a small, frightened-looking woman with watery eyes and a nervous habit of plucking at her pale lips with her fingers. Maher-shalal-hashbaz was released from his basket in the sitting-room, where Mr. Doe was reclining in an armchair, reading the evening paper. The cat sniffed suspiciously at him, but softened to Mrs. Doe's timid advances so far as to allow his ears to be tickled.

"Well, my dear," said Mr. Doe, "will he do? You don't object to the colour, eh?"

"Oh, no. He's a beautiful cat. I like him very much."

"Right. Then we'll take him. Here you are, Miss Maitland. Ten shillings. Please sign this receipt. Thanks. Never mind about the change from the half-crown. There you are, my dear; you've got your cat, and I hope we shall see no more of those mice. Now"—he glanced at his watch—"I'm afraid you must say good-bye to your pet quickly, Miss Maitland; we've got to get off. He'll be quite safe with us."

Monty strolled out with gentlemanly reticence into the hall while the last words were said. It was, no doubt, the same gentlemanly feeling which led him to move away from the sitting-room door towards the back part of the house; but he had only waited a very few minutes when Jean Maitland came out, sniffing valiantly into a small handkerchief, and followed by Mrs. Doe.

"You're fond of your cat, aren't you, my dear? I do hope you don't feel too—"

"There, there, Flossie," said her husband, appearing suddenly at her shoulders, "Miss Maitland knows he'll be well looked after." He showed them out, and shut the door quickly upon them.

"If you *don't* feel happy about it," said Mr. Egg uneasily, "we'll have him back in two twos."

"No, it's all right," said Jean. "If you don't mind, let's get in at once and drive away—rather fast."

As they lurched over the uneven road, Mr. Egg saw a lad coming down it. In one hand he carried a basket. He was whistling loudly.

"Look!" said Monty. "One of our hated rivals. We've got in ahead of him, anyhow. 'The salesman first upon the field gets the bargain signed and sealed.' Damn it!" he added to himself, as he pressed down the accelerator, "I *hope* it's O.K. I wonder."

Although Mr. Egg had worked energetically to get Maher-shalal-hashbaz settled in the world, he was not easy in his mind. The matter preyed upon his spirits to such an extent that, finding himself back to London on the following Saturday week, he made an expedition south of the Thames to make inquiries. And when the Maitland's door was opened by Jean, there by her side, arching his back and brandishing his tail, was Maher-shalal-hashbaz.

"Yes," said the girl, "he found his way back, the clever darling! Just a week ago to-day—and he was dreadfully thin and draggled—how he did it, I can't think. But we simply couldn't send him away again, could we, Maggie?"

"No," said Mrs. Maitland. "I don't like the cat, and never did, but there! I suppose even cats have their feelings. But it's an awkward thing about the money."

"Yes," said Jean. "You see, when he got back and we decided to keep him, I wrote to Mr. Doe and explained, and sent him a postal order for the ten shillings. And this morning the letter came back from the Post Office, marked 'Not Known.' So we don't know what to do about it."

"I never did believe in Mr. John Doe," said Monty. "If you ask me, Miss Maitland, he was no good, and I shouldn't bother any more about him."

But the girl was not satisfied, and presently the obliging Mr. Egg found himself driving out northwards in search of the mysterious Mr. Doe, carrying the postal order with him.

The door of the villa was opened by a neatly dressed,

elderly woman whom he had never seen before. Mr. Egg inquired for Mr. John Doe.

"He doesn't live here. Never heard of him."

Monty explained that he wanted the gentleman who had purchased the cat.

"Cat?" said the woman. Her face changed. "Step inside, will you? George!" she called to somebody inside the house, "here's a gentleman called about a cat. Perhaps you'd like to—" The rest of the sentence was whispered into the ear of a man who emerged from the sitting-room, and who appeared to be, and was in fact, her husband.

George looked Mr. Egg carefully up and down. "I don't know nobody here called Doe," said he; "but if it's the late tenant you're wanting, they've left. Packed and went off in a hurry the day after the old gentleman was buried. I'm the caretaker for the landlord. And if you've missed a cat, maybe you'd like to come and have a look out here."

He led the way through the house and out at the back door into the garden. In the middle of one of the flower-beds was a large hole, like an irregularly shaped and shallow grave. A spade stood upright in the mould. And laid in two lugubrious rows upon the lawn were the corpses of some very dead cats. At a hasty estimate, Mr. Egg reckoned that there must be close on fifty of them.

"If any of these is yours," said George, "you're welcome to it. But they ain't in what you might call good condition."

"Good Lord!" said Mr. Egg, appalled, and thought with pleasure of Maher-shalal-hashbaz, tail erect, welcoming him on the Maitland's threshold. "Come back and tell me about this. It's—it's unbelievable!"

It turned out that the name of the late tenants had been Proctor. The family consisted of an old Mr. Proctor, an invalid, to whom the house belonged, and his married nephew and the nephew's wife.

"They didn't have no servant sleeping in. Old Mrs. Crabbe used to do for them, coming in daily, and she always told me that the old gentleman couldn't abide cats. They made him ill like—I've known folks like that afore. And, of course, they had to be careful, him being so frail and his heart so bad he

148

might have popped off any minute. What it seemed to us when I found all them cats buried, like, was as how maybe young Proctor had killed them to prevent the old gentleman seeing 'em and getting a shock. But the queer thing is that all them cats looks to have been killed about the same time, and not so long ago, neither."

Mr. Egg remembered the advertisement, and the false name, and the applicants passed out by a different door, so that none of them could possibly tell how many cats had been bought and paid for. And he remembered also the careful injunction to bring the cat at 6 o'clock precisely, and the whistling lad with the basket who had appeared on the scene about a quarter of an hour after them. He remembered another thing— a faint miauling noise that had struck upon his ear as he stood in the hall while Jean was saying good-bye to Maher-shalal-hashbaz, and the worried look on Mrs. Proctor's face when she had asked if Jean was fond of her pet. It looked as though Mr. Proctor junior had been collecting cats for some rather sinister purpose. Collecting them from every quarter of London. From quarters as far apart as possible—or why so much care to take down names and addresses?

"What did the old gentleman die of?" he asked.

"Well," said Mrs. George, "it was just heart-failure, or so the doctor said. Last Tuesday week he passed away in the night, poor soul, and Mrs. Crabbe that laid him out said he had a dreadful look of horror on his poor face, but the doctor said that wasn't anything out of the way, not with his disease. But what the doctor didn't see, being too busy to come round, was them terrible scratches on his face and arms. Must have regular clawed himself in his agony—oh, dear, oh, dear! But there! Anybody knew as he might go off at any time like the blowing out of a candle."

"I know that, Sally," said her husband. "But what about them scratches on the bedroom door? Don't tell me he did that, too. Or, if he did, why didn't somebody hear him and come along to help him? It's all very well for Mr. Timbs— that's the landlord—to say as tramps must have got into the house after the Proctors left, and put us in here to look after the place, but why should tramps go for to do a useless bit of damage like that?"

"A 'eartless lot, them Proctors, that's what I say," said Mrs. George. "A-snoring away, most likely, and leaving their uncle to die by himself. And wasn't the lawyer upset about it, neither! Coming along in the morning to make the old gentleman's will, and him passed away so sudden. And seeing they came in for all his money after all, you'd think they might have given him a better funeral. Mean, I call it—not a flower, hardly—only one half-guinea wreath—and no oak—only elm and a shabby lot of handles. Such trash! You'd think they'd be ashamed."

Mr. Egg was silent. He was not a man of strong imagination, but he saw a very horrible picture in his mind. He saw an old, sick man asleep, and hands that quietly opened the bedroom door, and dragged in, one after the other, sacks that moved and squirmed and mewed. He saw the sacks left open on the floor, and the door being softly shut and locked on the outside. And then, in the dim glow of the night-light, he saw shadowy shapes that leapt and flitted about the room—black and tabby and ginger—up and down, prowling on noiseless feet, thudding on velvet paws from tables and chairs. And then, plump up on the bed—a great ginger cat with amber eyes—and the sleeper waking with a cry—and after that a nightmare of terror and disgust behind the locked and remorseless door. A very old, sick man, stumbling and gasping for breath, striking out at the shadowy horrors that pursued and fled him—and the last tearing pain at the heart when merciful death overtook him. Then, nothing but a mewing of cats and a scratching at the door, and outside, the listener, with his ear bent to the keyhole.

Mr. Egg passed his handkerchief over his forehead; he did not like his thoughts. But he had to go on, and see the murderer sliding through the door in the morning—hurrying to collect his innocent accomplices before Mrs. Crabbe should come—knowing that it must be done quickly and the corpse made decent—and that when people came to the house there must be no mysterious miaulings to surprise them. To set the cats free would not be enough—they might hang about the house.

No; the water-butt and then the grave in the garden. But Maher-shalal-hashbaz—noble Maher-shalal-hashbaz had fought for his life. He was not going to be drowned by any water-butts. He had kicked himself loose ("and I hope," thought Mr. Egg, "he scratched him all to blazes"), and he had toiled his way home across London. If only Maher-shalal-hashbaz could tell what he knew! But Monty Egg knew something, and he could tell.

"And I *will* tell, what's more," said Monty Egg to himself, as he wrote down the name and address of Mr. Proctor's solicitor. He supposed it must be murder to terrify an old man to death; he was not sure, but he meant to find out. He cast about in his mind for a consoling motto from the *Salesman's Handbook*, but, for the first time in his life, could find nothing that really fitted the case.

"I seem to have stepped regularly out of my line," he thought sadly; "but still, as a citizen—"

And then he smiled, recollecting the first and last aphorism in his favourite book:

> *To serve the Public is the aim*
> *Of every salesman worth the name*

Part Three

OTHER STORIES

◆

CHAPTER I

•

The Man Who Knew How

For perhaps the twentieth time since the train had left Carlisle, Pender glanced up from *Murder at the Manse* and caught the eye of the man opposite.

He frowned a little. It was irritating to be watched so closely, and always with that faint, sardonic smile. It was still more irritating to allow oneself to be so much disturbed by the smile and the scrutiny. Pender wrenched himself back to his book with a determination to concentrate upon the problem of the minister, murdered in the library. But the story was of the academic kind that crowds all its exciting incidents in the first chapter, and proceeds thereafter by a long series of deductions to a scientific solution in the last. The thin thread of interest, spun precariously upon the wheel of Pender's reasoning brain, had been snapped. Twice he had to turn back to verify points that he had missed in reading. Then he became aware that his eyes had followed three closely argued pages without conveying anything whatever to his intelligence. He was not thinking about the murdered minister at all—he was becoming more and more actively conscious of the other man's face. A queer face, Pender thought.

There was nothing especially remarkable about the features in themselves; it was their expression that daunted Pender. It was a secret face, the face of one who knew a great deal to other people's disadvantage. The mouth was a little crooked and tightly tucked in at the corners, as though savoring a hidden amusement. The eyes, behind a pair of rimless pince-nez, glittered curiously; but that was possibly due to the light reflected in the glasses. Pender wondered what the man's profession might be. He was dressed in a dark lounge suit, a raincoat and a shabby soft hat; his age was perhaps about forty.

Pender coughed unnecessarily and settled back into his corner, raising the detective story high before his face, barrier-fashion. This was worse than useless. He gained the impression that the man saw through the manœuvre and was secretly entertained by it. He wanted to fidget, but felt obscurely that his doing so would in some way constitute a victory for the other man. In his self-consciousness he held himself so rigid that attention to his book became a sheer physical impossibility.

There was no stop now before Rugby, and it was unlikely that any passenger would enter from the corridor to break up this disagreeable *solitude à deux*. But something must be done. The silence had lasted so long that any remark, however trivial, would—so Pender felt—burst upon the tense atmosphere with the unnatural clatter of an alarm clock. One could, of course, go out into the corridor and not return, but that would be an acknowledgment of defeat. Pender lowered *Murder at the Manse* and caught the man's eye again.

"Getting tired of it?" asked the man.

"Night journeys are always a bit tedious," replied Pender, half relieved and half reluctant. "Would you like a book?"

He took *The Paper-Clip Clue* from his attaché-case and held it out hopefully. The other man glanced at the title and shook his head.

"Thanks very much," he said. "but I never read detective stories. They're so—inadequate, don't you think so?"

"They are rather lacking in characterisation and human interest, certainly," said Pender, "but on a railway journey—"

"I don't mean that," said the other man. "I am not concerned with humanity. But all these murderers are so incompetent—they bore me."

"Oh, I don't know," replied Pender. "At any rate they are usually a good deal more imaginative and ingenious than murderers in real life."

"Than the murderers who are found out in real life, yes," admitted the other man.

"Even some of those did pretty well before they got pinched," objected Pender. "Crippen, for instance; he need never have been caught if he hadn't lost his head and run off to America. George Joseph Smith did away with at least two

156

brides quite successfully before fate and the *News of the World* intervened."

"Yes," said the other man, "but look at the clumsiness of it all; the elaboration, the lies, the paraphernalia. Absolutely unnecessary."

"Oh come!" said Pender. "You can't expect committing a murder and getting away with it to be as simple as shelling peas."

"Ah!" said the other man. "You think that, do you?"

Pender waited for him to elaborate this remark, but nothing came of it. The man leaned back and smiled in his secret way at the roof of the carriage; he appeared to think the conversation not worth going on with. Pender, taking up his book again, found himself attracted by his companion's hands. They were white and surprisingly long in the fingers. He watched them gently tapping upon their owner's knee—then resolutely turned a page—then put the book down once more and said:

"Well, if it's so easy, how would *you* set about committing a murder?"

"I?" repeated the man. The light on his glasses made his eyes quite blank to Pender, but his voice sounded gently amused. "That's different; *I* should not have to think twice about it."

"Why not?"

"Because I happen to know how to do it."

"Do you indeed?" muttered Pender, rebelliously.

"Oh, yes; there's nothing in it."

"How can you be sure? You haven't tried, I suppose?"

"It isn't a case of trying," said the man. "There's nothing tentative about my method. That's just the beauty of it."

"It's easy to say that," retorted Pender, "but what *is* this wonderful method?"

"You can't expect me to tell you that, can you?" said the other man, bringing his eyes back to rest on Pender's. "It might not be safe. You look harmless enough, but who could look more harmless than Crippen? Nobody is fit to be trusted with *absolute* control over other people's lives."

"Bosh!" exclaimed Pender. "I shouldn't think of murdering anybody."

"Oh, yes, you would," said the other man, "if you really

believed it was safe. So would anybody. Why are all these tremendous artificial barriers built up around murder by the Church and the law? Just because it's everybody's crime, and just as natural as breathing."

"But that's ridiculous!" cried Pender, warmly.

"You think so, do you? That's what most people would say. But I wouldn't trust 'em. Not with sulphate of thanatol to be brought for twopence at any chemist's."

"Sulphate of what?" asked Pender sharply.

"Ah! you think I'm giving something away. Well, it's a mixture of that and one or two other things—all equally ordinary and cheap. For ninepence you could make up enough to poison the entire Cabinet—and even you would hardly call that a crime, would you? But of course one wouldn't polish the whole lot off at once; it might look funny if they all died simultaneously in their baths."

"Why in their baths?"

"That's the way it would take them. It's the action of the the water that brings on the effect of the stuff, you see. Any time from a few hours to a few days after administration. It's quite a simple chemical reaction and it couldn't possibly be detected by analysis. It would just look like heart failure."

Pender eyed him uneasily. He did not like the smile; it was not only derisive, it was smug, it was almost—gloating—triumphant! He could not quite put a name to it.

"You know," pursued the man, thoughtfully pulling a pipe from his pocket and beginning to fill it, "it is very odd how often one seems to read of people being found dead in their baths. It must be a very common accident. Quite temptingly so. After all, there is a fascination about murder. The thing grows upon one—that is, I imagine it would, you know."

"Very likely," said Pender.

"Look at Palmer. Look at Gesina Gottfried. Look at Armstrong. No, I wouldn't trust anybody with that formula—not even a virtuous young man like yourself."

The long white fingers tamped the tobacco firmly into the bowl and struck a match.

"But how about you?" said Pender, irritated. (Nobody cares

158

to be called a virtuous young man.) "If nobody is fit to be trusted—"

"I'm not, eh?" replied the man. "Well, that's true, but it's past praying for now, isn't it? I know the thing and I can't unknow it again. It's unfortunate, but there it is. At any rate you have the comfort of knowing that nothing disagreeable is likely to happen to *me*. Dear me! Rugby already. I get out here. I have a little bit of business to do at Rugby."

He rose and shook himself, buttoned his raincoat about him and pulled the shabby hat more firmly down above his enigmatic glasses. The train slowed down and stopped. With a brief good-night and a crooked smile the man stepped on to the platform. Pender watched him stride quickly away into the drizzle beyond the radius of the gas-light.

"Dotty or something," said Pender, oddly relieved. "Thank goodness, I seem to be going to have the carriage to myself."

He returned to *Murder at the Manse*, but his attention still kept wandering.

"What was the name of that stuff the fellow talked about?" For the life of him he could not remember.

It was on the following afternoon that Pender saw the news-item. He had bought the *Standard* to read at lunch, and the word "Bath" caught his eye; otherwise he would probably have missed the paragraph altogether, for it was only a short one.

WEALTHY MANUFACTURER DIES IN BATH
WIFE'S TRAGIC DISCOVERY

A distressing discovery was made early this morning by Mrs. John Brittlesea, wife of the well-known head of Brittlesea's Engineering Works at Rugby. Finding that her husband, whom she had seen alive and well less than an hour previously, did not come down in time for breakfast, she searched for him in the bath-room, where, on the door being broken down, the engineer was found lying dead in his bath, life having been extinct, according to the medical men, for half an hour. The cause of the death is pronounced to be heart failure. The deceased manufacturer...

"That's an odd coincidence," said Pender. "At Rugby. I should think my unknown friend would be interested—if he is still there, doing his bit of business. I wonder what his business is, by the way."

It is a very curious thing how, when once your attention is attracted to any particular set of circumstances, that set of circumstances seems to haunt you. You get appendicitis: immediately the newspapers are filled with paragraphs about statesmen suffering from appendicitis and victims dying of it; you learn that all your acquaintances have had it, or know friends who have had it, and either died of it, or recovered from it with more surprising and spectacular rapidity than yourself; you cannot open a popular magazine without seeing its cure mentioned as one of the triumphs of modern surgery, or dip into a scientific treatise without coming across a comparison of the vermiform appendix in men and monkeys. Probably these references to appendicitis are equally frequent at all times, but you only notice them when your mind is attuned to the subject. At any rate, it was in this way that Pender accounted to himself for the extraordinary frequency with which people seemed to die in their baths at this period.

The thing pursued him at every turn. Always the same sequence of events; the hot bath, the discovery of the corpse, the inquest; always the same medical opinion; heart failure following immersion in too-hot water. It began to seem to Pender that it was scarcely safe to enter a hot bath at all. He took to making his own bath cooler and cooler every day, until it almost ceased to be enjoyable.

He skimmed his paper each morning for headlines about baths before settling down to read the news; and was at once relieved and vaguely disappointed if a week passed without a hot-bath tragedy.

One of the sudden deaths that occurred in this way was that of a young and beautiful woman whose husband, an analytical chemist, had tried without success to divorce her a few months previously. The coroner displayed a tendency to suspect foul play, and put the husband through a severe cross-examination. There seemed, however, to be no getting behind the doctor's evidence. Pender, brooding fancifully over the improbable possible, wished, as he did every day of the week, that he could remember the name of that drug the man in the train had mentioned.

Then came the excitement in Pender's own neighborhood. An old Mr. Skimmings, who lived alone with a housekeeper in a street just round the corner, was found dead in his bathroom. His heart had never been strong. The housekeeper told the milkman that she had always expected something of the sort to happen, for the old gentleman would always take his bath so hot. Pender went to the inquest.

The housekeeper gave her evidence. Mr. Skimmings had been the kindest of employers, and she was heartbroken at losing him. No, she had not been aware that Mr. Skimmings had left her a large sum of money, but it was just like his goodness of heart. The verdict was Death by Misadventure.

Pender, that evening, went out for his usual stroll with the dog. Some feeling of curiosity moved him to go round past the late Mr. Skimmings's house. As he loitered by, glancing up at the blank windows, the garden-gate opened and a man came out. In the light of a street lamp, Pender recognised him at once.

"Hullo!" he said.

"Oh, it's you, is it?" said the man. "Viewing the site of the tragedy, eh? What do *you* think about it all?"

"Oh, nothing very much," said Pender. "I didn't know him. Odd, our meeting again like this."

"Yes, isn't it? You live near here, I suppose."

"Yes," said Pender; and then wished he hadn't. "Do you live in these parts too?"

"Me?" said the man. "Oh, no. I was only here on a little matter of business."

"Last time we met," said Pender, "you had business at Rugby." They had fallen into step together, and were walking slowly down to the turning Pender had to take in order to reach his house.

"So I had," agreed the other man. "My business takes me all over the country. I never know where I may be wanted next."

"It was while you were at Rugby that old Brittlesea was found dead in his bath, wasn't it?" remarked Pender carelessly.

"Yes. Funny thing, coincidence." The man glanced up at him sideways through his glittering glasses. "Left all his money to his wife, didn't he? She's a rich woman now. Good-looking girl—a lot younger than he was."

They were passing Pender's gate. "Come in and have a drink," said Pender, and again immediately regretted the impulse.

The man accepted, and they went into Pender's bachelor study.

"Remarkable lot of these bath-deaths there have been lately, haven't there?" observed Pender carelessly, as he splashed soda into the tumblers.

"You think it's remarkable?" said the man, with his usual irritating trick of querying everything that was said to him. "Well, I don't know. Perhaps it is. But it's always a fairly common accident."

"I suppose I've been taking more notice on account of that conversation we had in the train." Pender laughed, a little self-consciously. "It just makes me wonder—you know how one does—whether anybody else had happened to hit on that drug you mentioned—what was its name?"

The man ignored the question.

"Oh, I shouldn't think so," he said. "I fancy I'm the only person who knows about that. I only stumbled on the thing by accident myself when I was looking for something else. I don't imagine it could have been discovered simultaneously in so many parts of the country. But all these verdicts just show, don't they, what a safe way it would be of getting rid of a person."

"You're a chemist, then?" asked Pender, catching at the one phrase which seemed to promise information.

"Oh, I'm a bit of everything. Sort of general utilityman. I do a good bit of studying on my own, too. You've got one or two interesting books here, I see."

162

Pender was flattered. For a man in his position—he had been in a bank until he came into that little bit of money—he felt that he had improved his mind to some purpose, and he knew that his collection of modern first editions would be worth money some day. He went over to the glass-fronted bookcase and pulled out a volume or two to show his visitor.

The man displayed intelligence, and presently joined him in front of the shelves.

"These, I take it, represent your personal tastes?" He took down a volume of Henry James and glanced at the fly-leaf. "That your name? E. Pender?"

Pender admitted that it was. "You have the advantage of me," he added.

"Oh! I am one of the great Smith clan," said the other with a laugh, "and work for my bread. You seem to be very nicely fixed here."

Pender explained about the clerkship and the legacy.

"Very nice, isn't it?" said Smith. "Not married? No. You're one of the lucky ones. Not likely to be needing any sulphate of . . . any useful drugs in the near future. And you never will, if you stick to what you've got and keep off women and speculation."

He smiled up sideways at Pender. Now that his hat was off, Pender saw that he had a quantity of closely curled grey hair, which made him look older than he had appeared in the railway carriage.

"No, I shan't be coming to you for assistance yet awhile," said Pender, laughing. "Besides, how should I find you if I wanted you?"

"You wouldn't have to," said Smith. "I should find you. There's never any difficulty about that." He grinned, oddly. "Well, I'd better be getting on. Thank you for your hospitality. I don't expect we shall meet again—but we may, of course. Things work out so queerly, don't they?"

When he had gone, Pender returned to his own armchair. He took up his glass of whisky, which stood there nearly full.

"Funny!" he said to himself. "I don't remember pouring

that out. I suppose I got interested and did it mechanically."
He emptied his glass slowly, thinking about Smith.

What in the world was Smith doing at Skimmings's house?

An odd business altogether. If Skimmings's housekeeper had known about that money. . . . But she had not known, and if she had, how could she have found out about Smith and his sulphate of . . . the word had been on the tip of his tongue then.

"You would not need to find me. I should find *you*." What had the man meant by that? But this was ridiculous. Smith was not the devil, presumably. But if he really had this secret— if he liked to put a price upon it—nonsense.

"Business at Rugby—a little bit of business at Skimmings's house." Oh, absurd!

"Nobody is fit to be trusted. *Absolute* power over another man's life . . . it grows on you."

Lunacy! And, if there was anything in it, the man was mad to tell Pender about it. If Pender chose to speak he could get the fellow hanged. The very existence of Pender would be dangerous.

That whisky!

More and more, thinking it over, Pender became persuaded that he had never poured it out. Smith must have done it while his back was turned. Why that sudden display of interest in the bookshelves? It had had no connection with anything that had gone before. Now Pender came to think of it, it had been a very stiff whisky. Was it imagination, or had there been something about the flavour of it?

A cold sweat broke out on Pender's forehead.

A quarter of an hour later, after a powerful dose of mustard and water, Pender was downstairs again, very cold and shivering, huddling over the fire. He had had a narrow escape— if he had escaped. He did not know how the stuff worked, but he would not take a hot bath again for some days. One never knew.

Whether the mustard and water had done the trick in time, or whether the hot bath was an essential part of the treatment, Pender's life was saved for the time being. But he was still uneasy. He kept the front door on the chain and warned his servant to let no strangers into the house.

He ordered two more morning papers and the *News of the World* on Sundays, and kept a careful watch upon their columns. Deaths in baths became an obsession with him. He neglected his first editions and took to attending inquests.

Three weeks later he found himself at Lincoln. A man had died of heart failure in a Turkish bath—a fat man, of sedentary habits. The jury added a rider to their verdict of Misadventure, to the effect that the management should exercise a stricter supervision over the bathers and should never permit them to be left unattended in the hot room.

As Pender emerged from the hall he saw ahead of him a shabby hat that seemed familiar. He plunged after it, and caught Mr. Smith about to step into a taxi.

"Smith," he cried, gasping a little. He clutched him fiercely by the shoulder.

"What, you again?" said Smith. "Taking notes of the case, eh? *Can I do anything for you?*"

"You devil!" said Pender. "You're mixed up in this! You tried to kill me the other day."

"Did I? Why should I do that?"

"You'll swing for this," shouted Pender menacingly.

A policeman pushed his way through the gathering crowd.

"Here!" said he, "what's all this about?"

Smith touched his forehead significantly.

"It's all right, officer," said he. "The gentleman seems to think I'm here for no good. Here's my card. The coroner knows me. But he attacked me. You'd better keep an eye on him."

"That's right," said a bystander.

"This man tried to kill me," said Pender.

The policeman nodded.

"Don't you worry about that, sir," he said. "You think better of it. The 'eat in there has upset you a bit. All right, *all* right."

"But I want to charge him," said Pender.

"I wouldn't do that if I was you," said the policeman.

"I tell you," said Pender, "that this man Smith has been

trying to poison me. He's a murderer. He's poisoned scores of people."

The policeman winked at Smith.

"Best be off, sir," he said. "I'll settle this. Now, my lad"—he held Pender firmly by the arms—"just you keep cool and take it quiet. That gentleman's name ain't Smith nor nothing like it. You've got a bit mixed up like."

"Well, what is his name?" demanded Pender.

"Never you mind," replied the constable. "You leave him alone, or you'll be getting yourself into trouble."

The taxis had driven away. Pender glanced round at the circle of amused faces and gave in.

"All right, officer," he said. "I won't give you any trouble. I'll come round with you to the police-station and tell you about it."

"What do you think o' that one?" asked the inspector of the sergeant when Pender had stumbled out of the station.

"Up the pole an' 'alf-way round the flag, if you ask me," replied his subordinate. "Got one o' them ideez fix what they talk about."

"H'm" replied the inspector. "Well, we've got his name and address. Better make a note of 'em. He might turn up again. Poisoning people so as they die in their baths, eh? That's a pretty good 'un. Wonderful how these barmy ones thinks it all out, isn't it?"

The spring that year was a bad one—cold and foggy. It was March when Pender went down to an inquest at Deptford, but a thick blanket of mist was hanging over the river as though it were November. The cold ate into your bones. As he sat in the dingy little court, peering through the yellow twilight of gas and fog, he could scarcely see the witnesses as they came to the table. Everybody in the place seemed to be coughing. Pender was coughing too. His bones ached, and he felt as though he were about due for a bout of influenza.

Straining his eyes, he thought he recognised a face on the other side of the room, but the smarting fog which penetrated every crack stung and blinded him. He felt in his overcoat pocket, and his hand closed comfortably on something thick and heavy. Ever since that day in Lincoln he had gone about armed for protection. Not a revolver—he was no hand with firearms. A sandbag was much better. He had bought one from an old man wheeling a barrow. It was meant for keeping out draughts from the door—a good, old-fashioned affair.

The inevitable verdict was returned. The spectators began to push their way out. Pender had to hurry now, not to lose sight of his man. He elbowed his way along, muttering apologies. At the door he almost touched the man, but a stout woman intervened. He plunged past her, and she gave a little squeak of indignation. The man in front turned his head, and the light over the door glinted on his glasses.

Pender pulled his hat over his eyes and followed. His shoes had crêpe rubber soles and made no sound on the sticking pavement. The man went on, jogging quietly up one street and down another, and never looking back. The fog was so thick that Pender was forced to keep within a few yards of him. Where was he going? Into the lighted streets? Home by 'bus or tram? No. He turned off to the left, down a narrow street.

The fog was thicker here. Pender could no longer see his quarry, but he heard the footsteps going on before him at the same even pace. It seemed to him that they were two alone in the world—pursued and pursuer, slayer and avenger. The street began to slope more rapidly. They must be coming out somewhere near the river.

Suddenly the dim shapes of the houses fell away on either side. There was an open space, with a lamp vaguely visible in the middle. The footsteps paused. Pender, silently hurrying after, saw the man standing close beneath the lamp, apparently consulting something in a notebook.

Four steps, and Pender was upon him. He drew the sandbag from his pocket. The man looked up.

"I've got you this time," said Pender, and struck with all his force.

Pender had been quite right. He did get influenza. It was a week before he was out and about again. The weather had changed, and the air was fresh and sweet. In spite of the weakness left by the malady he felt as though a heavy weight had been lifted from his shoulders. He tottered down to a favourite bookshop of his in the Strand, and picked up a D. H. Lawrence "first" at a price which he knew to be a bargain. Encouraged by this, he turned into a small chop-house, chiefly frequented by Fleet Street men, and ordered a grilled cutlet and a half-tankard of bitter.

Two journalists were seated at the next table.

"Going to poor old Buckley's funeral?" asked one.

"Yes," said the other. "Poor devil! Fancy his getting sloshed on the head like that. He must have been on his way down to interview the widow of that fellow who died in a bath. It's a rough district. Probably one of Jimmy the Card's crowd had it in for him. He was a great crime-reporter—they won't get another like Bill Buckley in a hurry."

"He was a decent sort, too. Great old sport. No end of a leg-puller. Remember his great stunt about sulphate of thanatol?"

Pender started. *That* was the word that had eluded him for so many months. A curious dizziness came over him and he took a pull at the tankard to steady himself.

". . . looking at you as sober as a judge," the journalist was saying. "He used to work off that wheeze on poor boobs in railway carriages to see how they'd take it. Would you believe that one chap actually offered him—"

"Hullo!" interrupted his friend. "That bloke over there has fainted. I thought he was looking a bit white."

CHAPTER II

•

The Fountain Plays

"Yes," said Mr. Spiller, in a satisfied tone, "I must say I like a bit of ornamental water. Gives a finish to the place."

"The Versailles touch," agreed Ronald Proudfoot.

Mr. Spiller glanced sharply at him, as though suspecting sarcasm, but his lean face expressed nothing whatever. Mr. Spiller was never quite at his ease in the company of his daughter's fiancé, though he was proud of the girl's achievement. With all his (to Mr. Spiller) unamiable qualities, Ronald Proudfoot was a perfect gentleman, and Betty was completely wrapped up in him.

"The only thing it wants," continued Mr. Spiller, "to *my* mind, that is, is Opening Up. To make a Vista, so to say. You don't get the Effect with these bushes on all four sides."

"Oh, I don't know, Mr. Spiller," objected Mrs. Digby in her mild voice. "Don't you think it makes rather a fascinating surprise? You come along the path, never dreaming there's anything behind those lilacs, and then you turn the corner and come suddenly upon it. I'm sure, when you brought me down to see it this afternoon, it quite took my breath away."

"There's that, of course," admitted Mr. Spiller. It occurred to him, not for the first time, that there was something very attractive about Mrs. Digby's silvery personality. She had distinction, too. A widow and widower of the sensible time of life, with a bit of money on both sides, might do worse than settle down comfortably in a pleasant house with half an acre of garden and a bit of ornamental water.

"And it's so pretty and secluded," went on Mrs. Digby, "with these glorious rhododendrons. Look how pretty they are, all sprayed with the water—like fairy jewels—and the rustic seat against those dark cypresses at the back. Really Italian. And the scent of the lilac is so marvellous!"

Mr. Spiller knew that the cypresses were, in fact, yews, but he did not correct her. A little ignorance was becoming in a woman. He glanced from the cotoneasters at one side of the fountain to the rhododendrons on the other, their rainbow flower-trusses sparkling with diamond drops.

"I wasn't thinking of touching the rhododendrons or the cotoneasters," he said. "I only thought of cutting through that great hedge of lilac, so as to make a vista from the house. But the ladies must always have the last word, mustn't they—er— Ronald?" (He never could bring out Proudfoot's Christian name naturally.) "If you like it as it is, Mrs. Digby, that settles it. The lilacs shall stay."

"It's too flattering of you," said Mrs. Digby, "but you mustn't think of altering your plans for me. I haven't any right to interfere with your beautiful garden."

"Indeed you have," said Mr. Spiller. "I defer to your taste entirely. You have spoken for the lilacs, and henceforward they are sacred."

"I shall be afraid to give an opinion on anything, after that," said Mrs. Digby, shaking her head. "But whatever you decide to do, I'm sure it will be lovely. It was a marvellous idea to think of putting the fountain there. It makes all the difference to the garden."

Mr. Spiller thought she was quite right. And indeed, though the fountain was rather flattered by the name of "ornamental water," consisting as it did of a marble basin set in the centre of a pool about four feet square, it made a brave show, with its plume of dancing water, fifteen feet high, towering over the smaller shrubs and almost overtopping the tall lilacs. And its cooling splash and tinkle soothed the ear on this pleasant day of early summer.

"Costs a bit to run, doesn't it?" demanded Mr. Gooch. He had been silent up till now, and Mrs. Digby felt that his remark betrayed a rather sordid outlook on life. Indeed, from the first moment of meeting Mr. Gooch, she had pronounced him decidedly common, and wondered that he should be on such intimate terms with her host.

"No, no," replied Mr. Spiller. "No, it's not expensive. You see, it uses the same water over and over again. Most ingenious. The fountains in Trafalgar Square work on the same principle, I believe. Of course, I had to pay a bit to have it put in, but I think it's worth the money."

"Yes, indeed," said Mrs. Digby.

"I always said you were a warm man, Spiller," said Mr. Gooch, with his vulgar laugh. "Wish I was in your shoes. A snug spot, that's what I call this place. Snug."

"I'm not a millionaire," answered Mr. Spiller, rather shortly. "But things might be worse in these times. Of course," he added, more cheerfully, "one has to be careful. I turn the fountain off at night, for instance, to save leakage and waste."

"I'll swear you do, you damned old miser," said Mr. Gooch, offensively.

Mr. Spiller was saved replying by the sounding of a gong in the distance.

"Ah! there's dinner," he announced, with a certain relief in his tone. The party wound their way out between the lilacs, and paced gently up the long crazy pavement, past the herbaceous borders and the two long beds of raw little ticketed roses, to the glorified villa which Mr. Spiller had christened "The Pleasaunce."

It seemed to Mrs. Digby that there was a slightly strained atmosphere about dinner, though Betty, pretty as a picture and very much in love with Ronald Proudfoot, made a perfectly charming little hostess. The jarring note was sounded by Mr. Gooch. He ate too noisily, drank far too freely, got on Proudfoot's nerves and behaved to Mr. Spiller with a kind of veiled insolence which was embarrassing and disagreeable to listen to. She wondered again where he had come from, and why Mr. Spiller put up with him. She knew little about him, except that from time to time he turned up on a visit to "The Pleasaunce," usually staying there about a month and being, apparently, well supplied with cash. She had an idea that he was some kind of commission agent, though she could not recall any distinct statement on this point. Mr. Spiller had settled down in the village about three years previously, and she had always liked him. Though not, in any sense of the word, a cultivated man, he was kind, generous and unassuming, and his devotion to Betty had something very lovable about it. Mr. Gooch had started coming about a year later. Mrs. Digby said to herself that if ever she was in a position to lay down the law at "The Pleasaunce"—and she had begun to think matters were tending that way—her influence would be directed to getting rid of Mr. Gooch.

"How about a spot of bridge?" suggested Ronald Proudfoot, when coffee had been served. It was nice, reflected Mrs. Digby, to have coffee brought in by the manservant. Masters was really a very well-trained butler, though he did combine the office with that of chauffeur. One would be comfortable at "The Pleasaunce." From the dining-room window she could see the neat garage housing the Wolseley saloon on the ground floor, with a room for the chauffeur above it, and topped off by a handsome gilded weather-vane a-glitter in the last rays of the sun. A good cook, a smart parlourmaid and everything done exactly as one could wish—if she were to marry Mr. Spiller she would be able, for the first time in her life, to afford a personal maid as well. There would be plenty of room in the house, and of course, when Betty was married—

Betty, she thought, was not over-pleased that Ronald had suggested bridge. Bridge is not a game that lends itself to the expression of tender feeling, and it would perhaps have looked better if Ronald had enticed Betty out to sit in the lilac-scented dusk under the yew-hedge by the fountain. Mrs. Digby was sometimes afraid that Betty was the more in love of the two. But if Ronald wanted anything he had to have it, of course, and personally, Mrs. Digby enjoyed nothing better than a quiet rubber. Besides, the arrangement had the advantage that it got rid of Mr. Gooch. "Don't play bridge," Mr. Gooch was wont to say. "Never had time to learn. We didn't play bridge where I was brought up." He repeated the remark now, and followed it up with a contemptuous snort directed at Mr. Spiller.

"Never too late to begin," said the latter pacifically.

"Not me!" retorted Mr. Gooch. "I'm going to have a turn in the garden. Where's that fellow Masters? Tell him to take the whisky and soda down to the fountain. The decanter, mind—one drink's no good to yours truly." He plunged a thick hand

172

into the box of Coronas on the side-table, took out a handful of cigars and passed out through the French window of the library on to the terrace. Mr. Spiller rang the bell and gave the order without comment, and presently they saw Masters pad down the long crazy path between the rose-beds and the herbaceous borders, bearing the whisky and soda on a tray.

The other four played on till 10:30, when, a rubber coming to an end, Mrs. Digby rose and said it was time she went home. Her host gallantly offered to accompany her. "These two young people can look after themselves for a moment," he added, with a conspiratorial smile.

"The young can look after themselves better than the old, these days." She laughed a little shyly, and raised no objection when Mr. Spiller drew her hand into his arm as they walked the couple of hundred yards to her cottage. She hesitated a moment whether to ask him in, but decided that a sweet decorum suited her style best. She stretched out a soft, beringed hand to him over the top of the little white gate. His pressure lingered—he would have kissed the hand, so insidious was the scent of the red and white hawthorns in her trim garden, but before he had summoned up courage, she had withdrawn it from his clasp and was gone.

Mr. Spiller, opening his own front door in an agreeable dream, encountered Masters.

"Where is everybody, Masters?"

"Mr. Proudfoot left five or ten minutes since, sir, and Miss Elizabeth has retired."

"Oh!" Mr. Spiller was a little startled. The new generation, he thought sadly, did not make love like the old. He hoped there was nothing wrong. Another irritating thought presented itself.

"Has Mr. Gooch come in?"

"I could not say, sir. Shall I go and see?"

"No, never mind." If Gooch had been sozzling himself up with whisky since dinner-time, it was just as well Masters should keep away from him. You never knew. Masters was one of these soft-spoken beggars, but he might take advantage. Better not to trust servants, anyhow.

"You can cut along to bed. I'll lock up."

"Very good, sir."

"Oh, by the way, is the fountain turned off?"

"Yes, sir. I turned it off myself, sir, at half-past ten, seeing that you were engaged, sir."

"Quite right. Good-night, Masters."

"Good-night, sir."

He heard the man go out by the back and cross the paved court to the garage. Thoughtfully he bolted both entrances, and returned to the library. The whisky decanter was not in its usual place—no doubt it was still with Gooch in the garden—but he mixed himself a small brandy and soda, and drank it. He supposed he must now face the tiresome business of getting Gooch up to bed. Then, suddenly, he realised that the encounter would take place here and not in the garden. Gooch was coming in through the French window. He was drunk, but not, Mr. Spiller observed with relief, incapably so.

"Well?" said Gooch.

"Well?" retorted Mr. Spiller.

"Had a good time with the accommodating widow, eh? Enjoyed yourself? Lucky old hound, aren't you? Fallen soft in your old age, eh?"

"There, that'll do," said Mr. Spiller.

"Oh, will it? That's good. That's rich. That'll do, eh? Think I'm Masters, talking to me like that?" Mr. Gooch gave a thick chuckle. "Well, I'm not Masters, I'm master here. Get that into your head. I'm master and you damn well know it."

"All right," replied Mr. Spiller meekly, "but buzz off to bed now, there's a good fellow. It's getting late and I'm tired."

"You'll be tireder before I've done with you." Mr. Gooch thrust both hands into his pockets and stood—a bulky and threatening figure—swaying rather dangerously. "I'm short of cash," he added. "Had a bad week—cleaned me out. Time you stumped up a bit more."

"Nonsense," said Mr. Spiller, with some spirit. "I pay you your allowance as we agreed, and let you come and stay here whenever you like, and that's all you get from me."

"Oh, is it? Getting a bit above yourself, aren't you, Number Bleeding 4132?"

"Hush!" said Mr. Spiller, glancing hastily round as though the furniture had ears and tongues.

"Hush! hush!" repeated Mr. Gooch mockingly. "You're in a good position to dictate terms, aren't you, 4132? Hush! The servants might hear! Betty might hear! Betty's young man might hear. Hah! Betty's young man—he'd be particularly pleased to know her father was an escaped jail-bird, wouldn't he? Liable at any moment to be hauled back to work out his ten years' hard for forgery? And when I think," added Mr. Gooch, "that a man like me, that was only in for a short stretch and worked it out good and proper, is dependent on the charity—ha, ha!—of my dear friend 4132, while he's rolling in wealth—"

"I'm not rolling in wealth, Sam," said Mr. Spiller, "and you know darn well I'm not. But I don't want any trouble. I'll do what I can, if you'll promise faithfully this time that you won't ask for any more of these big sums, because my income won't stand it."

"Oh, I'll promise that all right," agreed Mr. Gooch cheerfully. "You give me five thousand down—"

Mr. Spiller uttered a strangled exclamation.

"Five thousand? How do you suppose I'm to lay hands on five thousand all at once? Don't be an idiot, Sam. I'll give you a cheque for five hundred—"

"Five thousand," insisted Mr. Gooch, "or up goes the monkey."

"But I haven't got it," objected Mr. Spiller.

"Then you'd bloody well better find it," returned Mr. Gooch.

"How do you expect me to find all that?"

"That's your look-out. You oughtn't to be so damned extravagant. Spending good money, that you ought to be giving *me*, on fountains and stuff. Now, it's no good kicking, Mr. Respectable 4132—I'm the man on top and you're for it, my lad, if you don't look after me properly. See?"

Mr. Spiller saw only too clearly. He saw, as he had seen indeed for some time, that his friend Gooch had him by the short hairs. He expostulated again feebly, and Gooch replied with a laugh and an offensive reference to Mrs. Digby.

* * *

Mr. Spiller did not realise that he had struck very hard. He hardly realised that he had struck at all. He thought he had aimed a blow, and that Gooch had dodged it and tripped over the leg of the occasional table. But he was not very clear in his mind, except on one point. Gooch was dead.

He had not fainted; he was not stunned. He was dead. He must have caught the brass curb of the fender as he fell. There was no blood, but Mr. Spiller, exploring the inert head with anxious fingers, found a spot above the temple where the bone yielded to pressure like a cracked eggshell. The noise of the fall had been thunderous. Kneeling on the library floor, Mr. Spiller waited for the inevitable cry and footsteps from upstairs.

Nothing happened. He remembered—with difficulty, for his mind seemed to be working slowly and stiffly—that above the library there was only the long drawing-room, and over that the spare-room and bathrooms. No inhabited bedroom looked out on that side of the house.

A slow, grinding, grating noise startled him. He whisked round hastily. The old-fashioned grandfather clock, wheezing as the hammer rose into action, struck eleven. He wiped the sweat from his forehead, got up and poured himself out another, and a stiffer, brandy.

The drink did him good. It seemed to take the brake off his mind, and the wheels span energetically. An extraordinary clarity took the place of his previous confusion.

He had murdered Gooch. He had not exactly intended to do so, but he had done it. It had not felt to him like murder, but there was not the slightest doubt what the police would think about it. And once he was in the hands of the police— Mr. Spiller shuddered. They would almost certainly want to take his fingerprints, and would be surprised to recognise a bunch of old friends.

Masters had heard him say that he would wait up for Gooch. Masters knew that everybody else had gone to bed. Masters would undoubtedly guess something. But stop!

Could Masters prove that he himself had gone to bed? Yes, probably he could. Somebody would have heard him cross the court and seen the light go up over the garage. One could not hope to throw suspicion on Masters—besides, the man hardly deserved that. But the mere idea had started Mr. Spiller's brain on a new and attractive line of thought.

What he really wanted was an alibi. If he could only confuse the police as to the time at which Gooch had died. If Gooch could be made to seem alive after he was dead... somehow...

He cast his thoughts back over stories he had read on holiday, dealing with this very matter. You dressed up as the dead man and impersonated him. You telephoned in his name. In the hearing of the butler, you spoke to the dead as though he were alive. You made a gramophone record of his voice and played it. You hid the body, and thereafter sent a forged letter from some distant place—

He paused for a moment. Forgery—but he did not want to start that old game over again. And all these things were too elaborate, or else impracticable at that time of night.

And then it came to him suddenly that he was a fool. Gooch must not be made to live later, but to die earlier. He should die before 10:30, at the time when Mr. Spiller, under the eyes of three observers, had been playing bridge.

So far, the idea was sound and even, in its broad outline, obvious. But now one had to come down to detail. How could he establish the time? Was there anything that had happened at 10:30?

He helped himself to another drink, and then, quite suddenly, as though lit by a floodlight, he saw his whole plan, picked out vividly complete, with every join and angle clearcut.

He glanced at his watch; the hands stood at twenty minutes past eleven. He had the night before him.

He fetched an electric torch from the hall and stepped boldly out of the French window. Close beside it, against the wall of the house, were two taps, one ending in a nozzle for the garden hose, the other controlling the fountain at the bottom of the garden. This latter he turned on, and then, without troubling to muffle his footsteps, followed the crazy-paved path down to the lilac hedge, and round by the bed of cotoneasters. The sky, despite the beauty of the early evening, had now turned very dark, and he could scarcely see the tall column of pale water above the dark shrubbery, but he heard its comforting splash and ripple, and as he stepped upon the surrounding grass, he felt the blow spray upon his face. The beam of the torch showed him the garden seat beneath the yews, and the tray, as he had expected, standing upon it. The whisky decanter was about half full. He emptied the greater part of its contents into the basin, wrapping the neck of the decanter in his handkerchief, so as to leave no fingerprints. Then, returning to the other side of the lilacs, he satisfied himself that the spray of the fountain was invisible from house or garden.

The next part of the performance he did not care about. It was risky; it might be heard; in fact, he wanted it to be heard if necessary—but it was a risk. He licked his dry lips and called the dead man by name:

"Gooch! Gooch!"

No answer, except the splash of the fountain, sounding to his anxious ear abnormally loud in the stillness. He glanced round, almost as though he expected the corpse to stalk awfully out upon him from the darkness, its head hanging and its dark mouth dropping open to show the pale gleam of its dentures. Then, pulling himself together, he walked briskly back up the path and, when he reached the house again, listened. There was no movement, no sound but the ticking of the clocks. He shut the library door gently. From now on there must be no noise.

There was a pair of galoshes in the cloak-room near the pantry. He put them on and slipped like a shadow through the French window again: then round the house into the courtyard. He glanced up at the garage; there was no light in the upper story and he breathed a sigh of relief, for Masters was apt sometimes to be wakeful. Groping his way to an outhouse, he switched the torch on. His wife had been an invalid for some years before her death, and he had brought her wheeled chair with him to "The Pleasaunce," having a dim, sentimental reluctance to sell the thing. He was thankful for that, now; thankful, too, that he had purchased it from a good maker and that it ran so lightly and silently on its pneumatic tyres. He found the bicycle pump and blew the tyres up hard and, for further precaution, administered a drop of oil here and there.

Then, with infinite precaution, he wheeled the chair round to the library window. How fortunate that he had put down stone flags and crazy paving everywhere, so that no wheel-tracks could show.

The job of getting the body through the window and into the chair took it out of him. Gooch had been a heavy man, and he himself was not in good training. But it was done at last. Resisting the impulse to run, he pushed his burden gently and steadily along the narrow strip of paving. He could not see very well, and he was afraid to flash his torch too often. A slip off the path into the herbaceous border would be fatal; he set his teeth and kept his gaze fixed steadily ahead of him. He felt as though, if he looked back at the house, he would see the upper windows thronged with staring white faces. The impulse to turn his head was almost irresistible, but he determined that he would not turn it.

At length he was round the edge of the lilacs and hidden from the house. The sweat was running down his face and the most ticklish part of his task was still to do. If he broke his heart in the effort, he must carry the body over the plot of lawn. No wheel-marks or heel-marks or signs of dragging must be left for the police to see. He braced himself for the effort.

It was done. The corpse of Gooch lay there by the fountain, the bruise upon the temple carefully adjusted upon the sharp stone edge of the pool, one hand dragging in the water, the limbs disposed as naturally as possible, to look as though the man had stumbled and fallen. Over it, from head to foot, the water of the fountain sprayed, swaying and bending in the night wind. Mr. Spiller looked upon his work and saw that it was good. The journey back with the lightened chair was easy. When he had returned the vehicle to the outhouse and passed for the last time through the library window, he felt as though the burden of years had been rolled from his back.

His back! He had remembered to take off his dinner-jacket while stooping in the spray of the fountain, and only his shirt was drenched. That he could dispose of in the linen-basket, but the seat of his trousers gave him some uneasiness. He mopped at himself as best he could with his handkerchief. Then he made his calculations. If he left the fountain to play for an hour or so it would, he thought, produce the desired effect. Controlling his devouring impatience, he sat down and mixed himself a final brandy.

At 1 o'clock he rose, turned off the fountain, shut the library window with no more and no less than the usual noise and force, and went with firm footsteps up to bed.

Inspector Frampton was, to Mr. Spiller's delight, a highly intelligent officer. He picked up the clues thrown to him with the eagerness of a trained terrier. The dead man was last seen alive by Masters after dinner—8:30—just so. After which, the rest of the party had played bridge together till 10:30. Mr. Spiller had then gone out with Mrs. Digby. Just after he left, Masters had turned off the fountain. Mr. Proudfoot had left at 10:40 and Miss Spiller and the maids had then retired. Mr. Spiller had come in again at 10:45 or 10:50, and inquired for Mr. Gooch. After this, Masters had gone across to the garage, leaving Mr. Spiller to lock up. Later on, Mr. Spiller had gone down the garden to look for Mr. Gooch. He had gone no farther than the lilac hedge, and there calling to him and getting no answer, had concluded that his guest had already come in and gone to bed. The housemaid fancied she had heard him calling Mr. Gooch. She placed this episode at about half-past eleven—certainly not later. Mr. Spiller had subsequently sat up reading in the library till 1 o'clock, when he had shut the window and gone to bed also.

The body, when found by the gardener at 6:30 a.m., was still wet with the spray from the fountain, which had also soaked the grass beneath it. Since the fountain had been turned off at 10:30, this meant that Gooch must have lain there for an appreciable period before that. In view of the large quantity of whisky that he had drunk, it seemed probable that he had had a heart-attack, or had drunkenly stumbled, and, in falling, had struck his head on the edge of the pool. All these considerations fixed the time of death at from 9:30 to 10 o'clock—an opinion with which the doctor though declining to commit himself within an hour or so, concurred, and the coroner entered a verdict of accidental death.

* * *

Only the man who had been for years the helpless victim of blackmail could fully enter into Mr. Spiller's feelings. Compunction played no part in them—the relief was far too great. To be rid of the daily irritation of Gooch's presence, of his insatiable demands for money, of the perpetual menace of his drunken malice—these boons were well worth a murder. And, Mr. Spiller insisted to himself, as he sat musing on the rustic seat by the fountain, it had not really been murder. He determined to call on Mrs. Digby that afternoon. He could ask her to marry him now without haunting fear for the future. The scent of the lilac was intoxicating.

"Excuse me, sir," said Masters.

Mr. Spiller, withdrawing his meditative gaze from the spouting water, looked inquiringly at the manservant, who stood in a respectful attitude beside him.

"If it is convenient to you, sir, I should wish to have my bedroom changed. I should wish to sleep indoors."

"Oh?" said Mr. Spiller. "Why's that, Masters?"

"I am subject to be a light sleeper, sir, ever since the war, and I find the creaking of the weather-vane very disturbing."

"It creaks, does it?"

"Yes, sir. On the night that Mr. Gooch sustained his unfortunate accident, sir, the wind changed at a quarter past eleven. The creaking woke me out of my first sleep, sir, and disturbed me very much."

A coldness gripped Mr. Spiller at the pit of the stomach. The servant's eyes, in that moment, reminded him curiously of Gooch. He had never noticed any resemblance before.

"It's a curious thing, sir, if I may say so, that, with the wind shifting as it did at 11:15, Mr. Gooch's body should have become sprayed by the fountain. Up till 11:15, the spray was falling on the other side, sir. The appearance presented was as though the body had been placed in position subsequently to 11:15, sir, and the fountain turned on again."

"Very strange," said Mr. Spiller. On the other side of the lilac hedge, he heard the voices of Betty and Ronald Proudfoot, chattering as they paced to and fro between the herbaceous borders. They seemed to be happy together. The whole house seemed happier, now that Gooch was gone.

"Very strange indeed, sir. I may add that, after hearing the inspector's observations, I took the precaution to dry your dress-trousers in the linen-cupboard in the bathroom."

"Oh, yes," said Mr. Spiller.

"I shall not, of course, mention the change of wind to the authorities, sir, and now that the inquest is over, it is not likely to occur to anybody, unless their attention should be drawn to it. I think, sir, all things being taken into consideration, you might find it worth your while to retain me permanently in your service at—shall we say double my present wage to begin with?"

Mr. Spiller opened his mouth to say, "Go to Hell," but his voice failed him. He bowed his head.

"I am much obliged to you, sir," said Masters, and withdrew on silent feet.

Mr. Spiller looked at the fountain, with its tall water wavering and bending in the wind.

"Ingenious," he muttered automatically, "and it really costs nothing to run. It uses the same water over and over again."

There's an epidemic with 27 million victims. And no visible symptoms.

It's an epidemic of people who can't read.

Believe it or not, 27 million Americans are functionally illiterate, about one adult in five.

The solution to this problem is you... when you join the fight against illiteracy. So call the Coalition for Literacy at toll-free **1-800-228-8813** and volunteer.

**Volunteer
Against Illiteracy.
The only degree you need
is a degree of caring.**

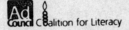

Ad Council Coalition for Literacy